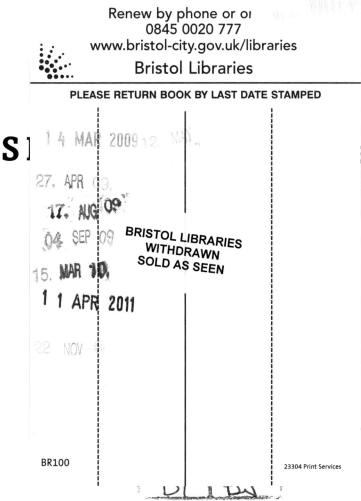

BRISTOL
REVIEW OF BOOKS

Bi   HC
      11/13

BRISTOL
SHORT STORY PRIZE
ANTHOLOGY

First published in 2008 by Bristol Review of Books Ltd,
81g Pembroke Rd Bristol BS8 3EA

www.bristolprize.co.uk
www.brbooks.co.uk

ISBN: 978-0-9559555-0-1

Cover designed by Femke de Jong; text designed by
Martin Laurie and printed by Latimer Trend Printers,
Exeter, Devon

Contents

Acknowledgements

The commitment and warm-hearted, unpaid support of numerous people has been instrumental in ensuring the success of the inaugural Bristol Short Story Prize.

The backing of the Prize by Waterstone's, Bristol Galleries and their generous contribution to the prizes has added immensely to the viability of the competition, as has the promotional support offered by Waterstone's as a whole. We would like to thank Zoe Hall, in particular, for all her encouragement and generosity, and also Mel Harris, Jo James and Janine Cook.

The expertise, integrity and commitment of the judging panel not only increased the prestige of the competition but also ensured the fairest possible judging process – a big thank you to Sara Davies, Patricia Ferguson, Nik Kalinowski and Joe Spurgeon for giving up their time so freely and willingly and also to the Zen-like calm of the chair, Mike Manson.

We would also like to thank Dr Paul Gough, Pro-Vice Chancellor of UWE, Christine Hill, Programme Leader of the UWE BA (Hons) Illustration course with Jonathan Ward and Gary Embury, and the final-year students at UWE for taking part in a competition to select the cover for this first anthology. Our warmest congratulations to Femke de Jong, whose design was chosen from a superb array of entries.

The patience and efficiency of our web-site designers made and continue to make a potentially difficult area a great pleasure – many thanks to Pete Morgan and Mark Furnevall of Sunspace Ltd., and to Joe Burt for his excellent designs for our flyers and logo, which gave the Prize a huge boost from the start.

Lu Hersey's help with all aspects of the competition was indispensable.

Many thanks also to the readers and administrators from the *Bristol Review of Books* editorial board, without whom the Prize would never have got off the ground, and in particular to Angela Sansom for her kind and patient efficiency, also to Sophie Collard, Fran Ham, Katherine Hanks and Helen Hart.

Joe Melia, *Prize co-ordinator*

Introduction

Welcome to the first *Bristol Short Story Prize Anthology*. This book is a celebration of new and emerging talent and presents the best and most innovative entries for the 2008 Bristol Short Story Prize. I'm sure you will enjoy it.

Even in the face of competition from the internet, podcasts, blogs and other new media, interest in reading has never been greater. Across the country people regularly gather in book groups to discuss their favourite novels. The desire to write is also strong. In Bristol every other person I meet seems to be writing a book – or at least thinking about writing one. (Not exactly the same thing!)

With this in mind the editors of the *Bristol Review of Books* got together with the Bristol Galleries branch of Waterstone's, who were pleased to sponsor this first Bristol Short Story Prize, its aim being to give aspiring and established writers a new showcase for their work.

While we knew creative writing was popular, the number of people putting finger to keyboard was a great deal higher than we anticipated. So much so that our loyal postman asked to be transferred to a different round! Writers' group spoke to writers' group through the web and soon, amazingly, entries arrived from across the UK and around the world. We received stories from Belgium, Bhutan, Canada, Denmark, Finland, France, Germany, Iran, Ireland, Italy, Japan, New Zealand, Portugal, Sicily, South Africa, Spain, Sri Lanka, Switzerland, U.S.A. and the United Arab Emirates.

The judges were hoping to read stories in a range of innovative styles. We were open to a broad interpretation of what a short story looks like. It didn't necessarily have to have a beginning, middle and end. It didn't have to be 3,000 words. In fact there was no lower word limit. In the end the format of the prose we received was largely traditional.

The judging was never going to be easy and coming to a consensus was bound to be fraught. Although we were all looking for a well-crafted story full of originality, the personal preferences of the judges nevertheless played a major role. And rightly so.

Did any overall themes emerge? The mood was apocalyptic. Reading the stories was not always an uplifting experience: tales of illness, mental disturbance, old age, death and suicide were recurring themes. Personally, I longed for the occasional story that would make me laugh. Or smile even. If, as somebody once said, writing is therapy for the author, at times it did feel that the judges had assumed the role of long-distance counsellors.

That comment aside, the task of judging was an honour and a pleasure. I glimpsed many weird and wonderful worlds. I was never sure which roller coaster I was on. Or where it would take me.

If you didn't make the 2008 Anthology don't despair. The Bristol Short Story Prize will be back next year. Keep an eye on the website www.bristolprize.co.uk for details. Loyal postman, you have been warned!

Mike Manson
Chair of Judges, 2008 Bristol Short Story Prize

A Judge's View

Hard-hearted murder, pitiful suicide, marital violence, apathetic old age... the darkest alcoves of human anguish ferociously seized and elegantly condensed into a breathless 3,000 words or less.

And all this, a mere three entries in. The immense task of judging this inaugural short story competition – dreamt up, and won, rather hearteningly, in a small corner of Bristol – loomed large, and somewhat bleak, from the beginning. But from the long-listed 40, the swirling journey proved to be one of much broader pleasures, and one wholly worth revisiting as the collection unpacked its frequently comical and deeply affecting contents, whisking us around the world and further still across that crooked axis defining our grasp on what it means to be human... from the hauntingly protracted agony of a childhood game in Catherine Chanter's 'The Boys Guide to Winning...' to the spectral, otherworldly fable integral to Derek Sellen's 'Angel and Assassin' to, most triumphantly, the tender eloquence of a wrenching final farewell in Rebecca Lloyd's unforgettable 'The River'.

Did my fellow judges and I make the right decisions? Can you even begin to weigh up a sprightly string of bawdy rhymes with a sloshing dose of British nostalgia on the sands of Brean? Of course not. But with absolute certainty, within this deceptively slim volume, you'll find a line, a sense, a twist, an idea, a feast, confirming the strength of the short story – in a world besieged by the roaming, panoramic, media-courted novel – to be very much alive and in rather rampaging form. Take a breath, kick up the heels, uncover a hidden corner of stolen solitude and enjoy the ride.

Joe Spurgeon
Judge

The Bristol Short Story Prize is a collaboration between *The Bristol Review of Books* and Waterstone's (Bristol Galleries Branch).
The competition raises funds for the Bristol Review of Books.

Mike Manson (Chair)
Author, psychogeographer, contributing editor of the *Bristol Review of Books* and director of Past & Present Press. His novel *Where's My Money?* is published by Tangent Books. He is the Bristol Books and Publishers representative on the board of judges.

Sara Davies
Has been producing plays and arts programmes for BBC Radio 4 for over fifteen years, and has commissioned work from some of the country's best writers. She's also been delighted to find stories for broadcast by unknown and new writers. Before taking on this proper job, she had an eccentric career as a freelance journalist, television presenter, copywriter, teacher and market stallholder.

Patricia Ferguson
Has lived in Bristol for nearly twenty years, and has published five novels and a collection of short stories. Her first novel won the Somerset Maugham award, the David Higham award and the Betty Trask prize; her last two were both long-listed for the Orange Prize. She currently teaches Creative Writing at Bristol University.

Nik Kalinowski
Is a photographer and bookseller. An avid reader, especially of foreign fiction, he has travelled widely to Australia, America, Thailand and most of Europe. He recently co-wrote the literary reference guide *The Bloomsbury Good Reading Guide to World Fiction*.

Joe Spurgeon
Current editor of *Venue* magazine, having written previously as a freelancer across numerous dubious, slipshod and occasionally reputable publications, websites and anywhere else where someone gave him a typewriter and a brief, really. Avid fan of local puppetry, shortcrust pastry pies, Bristol's Gloucester Road and nerdy Phonogram comics.

Rebecca Lloyd

Rebecca's stories have been published in Canada, USA, New Zealand and the UK. She runs a creative writing course in the Grant Bradley Gallery in Bedminster, Bristol. She lives in a house once owned by the butcher poet of Bedminster. She hopes he regarded himself as a poet first and a butcher second - most writers have daytime jobs, but it helps to keep motivated if you regard your daytime job as 'the other thing you do.' She is the volunteer fundraiser for Fareshare SouthWest, a charity redistributing good food destined for landfill to organisations supporting people without access to healthy food otherwise.

The River

1st Prize

Rebecca Lloyd

I didn't know my grandfather had started fishing again until the landlord of The Ropemaker beckoned me one afternoon as I came home from work. 'I've banned him from the walkway. You should look after him better, Miss,' he warned me. 'He pulled up a whooper and my son had to help him with it. They lost it. The old geezer said he'd gladly have gone down with it.'

'Sounds like him,' I said. 'How big?'

'Girth of a drainpipe, apparently.'

Grandpa was on the balcony as I came in, looking down at the floating rubbish island that docked for a short while between our house and The Ropemaker. 'We never had rubbish like this at Tilbury,' he said.

'It's all the trash from the city, Grandpa.'

'Where do you think it goes?'

'Down to the sea, I expect. You were fishing again. You said you were done with it all.'

'Tide's coming in fast, look.'

At high tide, water slapped across our balcony floor and wetted the windows. In violent weather, you could feel its force as it struck the house wall below, and pulled away and struck again. There was a drop of twenty-five feet between tides, and at low tide, the foreshore was exposed for as far as we could see in either direction. We liked the sound of the river's brown waves rolling upwards as the tide came in again, they made the pebbles gleam, and deposited their foamy edges in a ridge of scum as they reached out again for the river walls.

'Next door said you were fishing.'

'I was just checking that there really are big fish up here so close to the city. That kid from the pub had an eel bucket. I was curious.'

I'd forgotten the long hours my grandfather spent alone. I stared at the scores of plastic milk bottles moving serenely amongst the rubbish. 'Did you eat something?'

'Couldn't open the biscuit packet. Could no more open the bloody thing than get out of my own coffin,' he muttered.

Grandpa used to dream about his death. I'd glimpse him sometimes through the patchy mirror above the stove when we got up in the morning, and terror was clear on his face. 'You can warp a persistent bad dream,' I'd told him. 'If you think about it angrily, you can take your anger back into the dream and change the course of it.'

'Is that so, Maggie?'

'Try it with the dreams you have. Tell yourself you just have to reach your hands up and push the lid off, and in a minute you'll be out and free.'

'Tell myself I'm not on fire alone in a dark place amid horrible music?'

'Tell yourself that before the coffin slides behind that creepy curtain that doesn't even sway, you burst out and run through the crematorium, laughing.'

'That'd be funny,' he said, but I could hear him thinking it wouldn't make a jot of difference to the real thing. He pretended it was working for a while; inventing moments in his dreams I suspected weren't true, 'I was flying above Tilbury and I could see the river below me, all glinting in the sun.'

'Yeah?'

'It was glorious. I flew in the vaults of the church and I could see figures below with their hands raised up, and they were all hissing with anger. Then I flew over our old house with the concrete yard and the outside toilet.'

'Really? But, Grandpa, when you die, you're free from that very moment. You don't know anything then.'

'Maggie, it's not deadness itself, it's how they fiddle and fuss, and what they do to you; they take away a man's uniqueness.'

'But you won't know.'

'I will. I know now, unless you can do something about it for me.'

I'd had a persistent dark dream about his death as well, one I didn't tell him about for fear he'd covet it. I sing in the dream desperately, but it makes no difference, the monster he caught when I was seven slithers off the bank with scarcely a ripple, taking him under the brown water with it.

I never did go down to the river with him again after the day he landed the creature, and a while ago he told me he'd regretted me being there too, 'It was a man to man thing, and you were only a wee girl.'

The smaller eels, bootlaces he called them, weighed only a few pounds, and when they wrapped themselves around his wrists like living bracelets, I'd thought it funny. My job was to make a groove in the earth by the bank. 'A bed for them,' he said, 'so they're all comfy when we get them up.'

When the big hit came, Grandpa got to his feet very quickly. I saw him brace his legs and straighten his back. He whistled low under his breath and muttered something. He gave no slack on the line, and three times the great eel headed fast for the rushes and he forced it out into the open again. 'Make the bed really big,' he called to me. I could feel my heart thumping against my knee as I scraped at the soft mud with my trowel. 'Make another groove through the middle so it's like a cross. Do it quick, Maggie.'

The backs of Grandpa's legs were trembling. He had the net ready, and the eel was close to it. It rose to the surface and thrashed its pointed head about, fighting hard and foaming up the water. Five times he nearly lost it, then, when he finally brought it to the bank, the fight between them escalated. Grandpa shouted and pleaded with the thing in turns. It thwacked violently in his grip and I thought he'd fall into the water with it. I backed away and looked towards the path, thinking to run home and hide.

Finally, he had it tight in both hands, holding it at arm's length, upside down. It was thicker than a lamppost, a great slimy pillar of silver-grey muscle. It seemed a long while before Grandpa moved again to lay it in the groove on its back. He beckoned me to crouch down beside him, and taking my trembling hand, showed me how to stroke it so it'd stay quiet. 'Talk to it, Maggie. Stroke it softly.'

I felt like crying. 'What'll I say, Grandpa?'

'Sing the hymn you learnt in school last week.'

'All Things Bright And Beautiful'?

'That's it. I've got to ease the hook out, and the man must stay very still so I don't harm him.'

I remember the sound of my thin voice singing on the wrong note, and the feel of my fingertips on the slime of the eel's belly. It wasn't deep-hooked and Grandpa was glad. 'See, Maggie,' he said, as he watched me work the creature, 'you don't have to be strong, or a man, to do something awesome in life.'

And that was it; that was, the feeling that had come upon me, if awe is a solemn quiet thing that reaches deep inside you.

'Why do you throw the big ones back, Grandpa?'

'Because they've come so far against the odds; three thousand miles from the Sargasso Sea. Mind you, no one's ever found an eel egg there.' He took the hook gently out of the animal's lip. 'This man's a toothy one, see? That means he hunts fish, and doesn't bother much with bloodworms and things.' He scooped the beast into his arms, and cradling it there for a moment, took it to the river's edge. As it slithered off the muddy bank and away into the water, I wiped my slimy fingers on my dress and Grandpa waved to it.

'I'm glad he's back, he looked all wrong out of the water.'

'Oh, you'd be surprised the places you find eels, and how far they can travel over land. They're gypsies. They're clever and free, not tied down like most people are, you know.'

On the night of the eclipse of the moon, I took the old armchair out of the living room and onto the balcony, and settled my grandfather in it with a blanket. 'A good night for eels,' he said.

'Grandpa, you remember when we got the big one, Why did I have to make two grooves for it?'

'Oh, I just got over excited. My own grandfather always made a cross for eels to get the devil out of them. They're not like other fish, they get anywhere where there's water.'

I remembered the great wriggling mass of muscle and the way Grandpa sighed when he took the hook out of its lip. 'How big do you reckon it was?'

'He must have had a twelve-inch girth, and I had him at about four foot. I've always wished I'd caught him at night. There's nothing like eel fishing in the moonlight. They go into the upper layers of water and the moon makes the small fish visible to them. You use a float then, and they're a sight to see swirling around the bait before they take it.'

'Did you do that Grandpa, fish at night?'

'Of course I did. They're nocturnal feeders, those men.'

'While I was asleep at home?'

He shrugged. 'Yes, sometimes.'

'Did you want to be free – like an eel?'

He laughed. 'Who wouldn't?'

'You left me at home. How often?'

'Oh, things were safe in those days, my love. It's not like now.'

'What is now like, Grandpa?'

He rocked forward for a moment and slumped back in his chair. I kept my eyes on the moon; it was brilliantly silver with grey countries all over it. 'It's meaner, Maggie, darker. When you get old, you can't be bothered with meanness and darkness because it's not your time anymore. But you don't want to mention it, because the ones you love, in my case the single one, have to go on living in it.'

My throat tightened. 'Was I a burden to you all those years after Mum and Dad died?'

'Don't be daft, Girl, you were the centre of everything for me, you and the men.'

'How often did you go out at night?'

'Well, you came with me at the weekends, didn't you? You seemed to enjoy it before I caught the big one. You were all queer and dreamy on the way home that day. I felt as if I didn't know who you were.'

'I sometimes feel as if I don't know you. How often?'

'Every night,' he whispered. 'Came back at dawn. There now.'

'Christ, Grandpa!'

'It's in my blood Maggie, eel fishing. I could never resist it.'

'Every night. I was a burden to you then.'

'It's hard bringing up a kid, Maggie. But you were no burden, not like I am to you now.'

'You're not, Grandpa. Don't think that.'

'Thank you, Maggie. But I've become a burden to myself.'

The moon was changing colour, dimming to a strange browny-red, and by the time we went inside it was hanging in the sky like a moist red grape.

The rubbish island came our way on the high tide at around four o'clock. The larger objects, lumps of polystyrene and wooden planks, gave the thing cohesion, between them floated plastic bottles of all kinds, and the lids from take-away cappuccinos. I never saw an island without a couple of footballs amongst the jumble, and a few shoes. The whole sad flotilla, a peculiar combination of the once cared-for and the utterly irrelevant, stayed together in the calm waters, and if disrupted by a wave thrown up suddenly by a speeding boat, formed as one mass again quickly, aided by the underwater currents.

It was as if each object, disengaged from its original purpose, found a new legitimacy in the great river, where in its kinship with other floating things it formed a forlorn mosaic about the lives of careless people. And objects that once had meaning, private things – shoes, baseball caps, the occasional jacket, gave the island a curious poignancy as they floated amongst the other trash.

'Why are you taking pictures of it, Maggie?'

I'd rather Grandpa had thought my work was to do with the light and the sky; I didn't think he'd understand my fascination with ordinary things in the wrong places. 'There's interesting stuff down there, Grandpa.'

He came to stand beside me. 'I suppose there is. Are people going to buy pictures of sunglasses and rubber sandals all bobbing and floating in the water like that?'

'I don't know yet.'

'Funny business, life.'

He became ill for a couple of weeks that spring and the last of his stamina and muscle fell away from him. I stayed at home and sat with him on the balcony. We played a game of trying to name the colours on the river before they changed. There were afternoons when the tiny choppy waves that signalled the incoming tide were yellow ochre at their crests in the low sunlight, and the writhing valleys of water between them were a war of deep blue and silver. Yet, you could turn away for a second and look again to find the waves had dulled to a translucent muddy brown, and the green algae on the river wall was no longer vivid.

He was as light as a cuttlefish bone, and I could've carried him easily through the rooms of the house if he'd allowed it. Instead, he shuffled painfully from one room to the other and out onto the balcony. It was fine weather. In the early morning, a silvery-blue light lay across the metal roofs of the factories on the other side of the river so they looked like slabs of molten metal, and the detail on all the buildings was obliterated in the haze so they became no more than giant cubes.

I took him out to walk on the foreshore at low tide, along the band of white sand against the river wall. Closer to the edge of the water the sand turned to fine grey silt dotted with half bricks from houses once standing along the shore. We could smell the sea the Thames finally reaches sometimes, and in the sunlight, the old bricks cast square shadows behind them on the wet mud.

Then quite suddenly one morning, my grandfather was gone. I checked the street and the local store. I called out for him stupidly, and finally went to The Ropemaker. The landlord hadn't seen him and he looked at me distantly and hopelessly.

At four o'clock that day, the son walked in through my open door and joined me on the balcony. 'No luck yet?' I shook my head. I'd fallen into a terrible dreaming state, a state of knowing and denying at the same time. Of all the people I might've wanted with me, this ugly youth with remote eyes that slid about and never rested, was not one.

The island submerged and surfaced languidly, pale. Two tennis balls, furry and light green, bobbed amongst the rubbish and a shoe floated sole upwards nearby. I noticed the second shoe emerge from beneath a slab of polystyrene, and as if by its own effort, turn itself over to mimic its partner. The water was dark, all its facets sombre, slate-grey and rippling. A shaft of sudden sunlight flung a field of silver across its surface and blurred the island's contents. No boats mangled the pattern of currents and ripples, no birds flew overhead. A plastic paint bucket, half sunk and half floating, moved amongst the sticks and bottles. As the sun dimmed, a face appeared within the island, a face and body, hands waxen.

The boy caught hold of my arm and I didn't pull away. 'It'll go down to the sea presently,' he murmured.

He was beautiful down there; the water had softened the sharp contours of his face, and his hair floated around him like fine weed. His hands were relaxed and his fingers spread open as if in a gesture of welcome. He'd put on his navy-blue suit, and his tie lay like a strap around his chin. One of his shoes had come off, and he hadn't bothered to put on any socks. A sodden trilby floated nearby with a feather in the headband, it wasn't Grandpa's, but he would've liked it.

'There was an old geezer in the water a couple of years ago,' the boy whispered, 'in the lower pool by Wapping.' I began to cry. 'Only in his case he didn't have no family. He had a purse on him, they said, and they found a note in it written in grammar. It said I am Shaun Peters. I have no relations.

'To my way of thinking Jimmy was a lucky man having you.' He let go of my arm and shuffled backwards as if he'd suddenly become aware of his intimacy with me.

The island began to creep out of the recess inch by inch as the currents changed. Grandpa floated in the midst of it, elegantly. I could feel my fingers bruising on the wooden rail. 'I don't know what to do.'

'Don't do nothing, Miss. He might make it to the open sea.'

I felt a sudden twist of anger. 'You didn't know my grandfather.'

'I did too. Him and me fished together most every afternoon.' His eyes were deep and steady, and on my face. 'He's me, only old. Don't disturb him now. He wants it this way. Look at him down there; it's like he's sleeping.'

The island swayed gently on its outward journey and Grandpa lay languid in the midst of it, and as I watched the beautiful serenity of the floating trash, I felt awe, if awe is a solemn quiet kind of thing that reaches deep inside you.

Derek Sellen

Derek lives in Canterbury, where he teaches and writes textbooks for foreign learners. He has been writing poetry, short stories and drama for many years and has been awarded prizes in various competitions and been included in PEN, Arts Council and other anthologies. He has read on the radio and given readings in Essen, Germany, and Novorossysk, Russia, as well as in the UK, while his plays have been performed in Brighton, the University of Kent and Bratislava. 'Angel and Assassin' started with some lines from Chaucer and then developed into a rather different kind of tale.

Angel and Assassin   *2nd Prize*

Derek Sellen

I have an angel which that loveth me,
That with greet love, wher-so I wake or slepe,
Is redy ay my body for to kepe.
from **The Second Nun's Tale**. Geoffrey Chaucer

1.

She was a professional challenge.

Cecilia was the saint that nobody could kill, the living martyr. The lions, starved for a week and goaded with lances, would not eat her. When she was placed in a bath of fire, the flames would not burn her. When they tried to hack off her head, the axe blade shied away from her neck. On the wheel, she did not break. Poison became sugared water in her veins. The rope slipped its knot and held her in a harness of love. Magistrates, jailers and executioners held no fear for her. She joined the holy calendar.

At the time I met her, she was nearly 1,800 years old.

You had to be crazy to believe that of course; but when it comes to faith, there are still enough people who live in the Middle Ages. The rest of us thought it was a lie of the scammers who had built up an organisation around her. These hangers-on called themselves the Sect Harmonious of the Immortal Virgin (SHIV, though I would have exchanged the final letter of that acronym) and peddled the

21

myth that chastity enables you to live forever. Certainly Cecilia had the attributes of youth – the unblemished, peach skin, the unjaded gaze, the glowing energy. Time had refused to act on her. Or else, as we assumed, this was some teenage impostor, persuaded to play the role her captors wanted her to, a fake cult goddess who was feigning immortality.

There was a mythical history attached to the cult. Cecilia had married Valerian in Roman times, persuaded him to Christianity and to marital abstinence. 'I have an angel,' she told him, 'who loves me well. He will show himself to you in joy and brightness if you do not touch me in our bed.'

Valerian saw the angel.

Then the persecution intensified. Her husband having been executed for his new faith, she was herself arraigned. She cheeked the magistrate, was placed in a fire but, miraculously surviving unharmed, had her throat slit and was left for dead, the blood draining away. This is where the stories fork.

But you don't have to believe in parallel universes to explain this; it can be explained simply by the nature of story-tellers, their unwillingness to let a good tale end. Although most agree that she died, a few claim that she survived even virtual decapitation with no more than a scarlet ring around the throat. She was spirited away by her followers and can be traced through the centuries.

A holy eremite in the Lebanon.

A virgin captured by pirates who, seduced by her eloquence, spared her alone out of a massacre of 700.

A prioress renowned for piety and a new strain of apples in a Norfolk nunnery.

A reclusive author of religious tracts.

A lady of good works in workhouses and paupers' hospitals.

Finally, she has transformed into this, our modern-day Cecilia who was 'identified' by the red circlet like a stitched wound at the base of her neck. She was found living rough among prostitutes and junkies, herself a virgin, kept since then by her captors in a nun's penthouse cell.

How do I know all this? I did my research. I'm not a sloppy worker.

I called them her 'captors' since that was what they were. She was held in an apartment at the top of their tall headquarters building, with guards on every floor, gates that required an electronic card to open across the stairways, elevators operated by a code-pad, cameras that scanned the approaches. All this was for her security, it was claimed, to maintain her purity, as if by breathing an air contaminated by the ordinary sweat and the ordinary exhalations of ordinary human beings she would be fatally damaged, but in reality it was done as much to keep *her* in as to keep others away.

There was a web-cam that relayed pictures of her every movement to a paying site on the Internet. There you could watch her, a distant figure in white, trapped in the ovoid eye of the camera. You saw her sleep and rise, eat and drink, sit in lotus-position meditation for hours, disappear off-screen to urinate or defecate, return, read, move her lips silently to camera – you never heard her voice but those believers who could lip-read said that she spoke words of comfort in fifty-seven languages to the watchers – bow her head in prayer, sometimes shuffle in a private dance of great grace, curl on a floor mat and sleep. She lived in absolute solitude; food and drink, petitions written on scrolls, changes of robe, supplies of necessities, were delivered through a hatch. Among the commonplace Internet images of displayed nakedness and celebrity titbits, Cecilia operated in a different mode.

Why, I wondered, did they not transmit her voice? Were they afraid that, given a microphone to the world, Saint Cecilia would broadcast her discontent with her imprisonment, publish some message that cracked the illusion of her holiness?

The job came through to me – a consortium of rival cult bosses were angered by the amount of adherents the Saint Cecilia fad was attracting, the overshadowing of their own pseudo-religious enterprises, the loss of revenue they were experiencing as a result. Economics dictated that the immortal virgin had to die.

It was not as easy as I could have wished; there was no clear line of sight from the rooftop parapet of any neighbouring building of the same height and in any case she lived behind perpetually shrouded windows. I had to get to her another way. The security seemed elaborate but in fact it was amateurish; they were guarding against cranks, not against a professional. To duck under the arc of a poorly positioned camera, to enter through a service door, to drug the off-duty guards, to steal one of their uniforms and a set of electronic cards, to ascend by stairway and lift while the on-duty guards gossiped, to reach her sanctum, all this was boringly simple. I stood, armed, outside her door.

I broke it down.

I shot out the cameras.

The webscreens of her adherents all over the world went black.

2.

What had I expected when I turned the gun from the cameras to sight it on her body? That the rapid fire would drill her from throat to groin, fountains of blood issuing as the bullets hit? Or that she would somehow survive as her cult members claimed she would? That an invisible shield would deflect the bullets or that she would palm them away as if they were paper pellets?

That an angel would swoop and pluck her out of danger?

No.

This is what happened. As I was in the act of firing, some force pushed the barrel of the gun to the side, turning it forty-five degrees, so that the bullets thudded into the empty corner of the room.

It took some moments for my conscious thoughts to catch up with what had been an instinctive action, to recognise the swerve of the weapon as something I had instigated myself, not a divine intervention. As I aimed, I had seen her face and as I had seen her face, I had flinched from the task and at the last possible instant swung the gun to the right. I had killed industrialists, a president and a priest, several leading politicians, a top scientist and various secret agents, both foreign and our own, anyone that I was paid to eliminate. But at the moment of assassination, the moment of professional consummation, my eyes saw something in the face of this girl which made my hands baulk.

Intelligence. Compassion. Spirit. All these and more. As if two thousand years of living had imprinted something as deep as time in the countenance of an eighteen-year-old girl.

'You're here,' she said.

'We're getting out,' I said.

3.

Saint Cecilia sat opposite me across a rough wooden table in the cellar, she in her hair shirt under her robe, I in my bullet-proof vest. I had not had to force her to accompany me, she had come willingly enough as if under some duty, dodging down the stairs as I shot at her pursuing guards and left them sprawled on the floor in fear or cowering against walls out of the spray of bullets. The cult proprietors appeared from office doors but she paid them no attention. They were not her kind of people either, the career preachers, the donation-pocketers, the door-to-door faith-hawkers, the redemption-mongers. They were summoners and pardoners all.

It had caused a big stir. My paymasters in this mission were not pleased. Instead of an immortal virgin who had been proved a fake by an assassin's bullet, there was a sensational kidnapping, a police search, daily publicity for the SHIV cult. I received urgent communications. She had to be killed, her body left to be discovered, with a placard attached proclaiming her a fraud, laying the blame on some disgruntled ex-believer who had seen through her trickery.

'You're causing me a lot of problems,' I told her.

It had not been necessary to bind her. She gave me her word that she did not intend to escape so long as I did not try to molest her sexually and I believed her.

'The trouble comes from you,' she told me now. 'If you do not have the courage to kill me as your employers want or the courage to disobey them, then we shall sit here in hiding for ever.'

'Courage? To kill you? I've killed eighty, ninety, a hundred. I don't count them any more.'

'Men? Women? Teenagers? Children?'

'They call me the machine,' I said. 'If a child is a witness to a killing, I kill the child too. You must approve of that. At least I leave no orphans.'

'You are full of pride,' she said.

I shrugged. 'I do my work well and efficiently. There are no complaints. It is not a question, as you said just now, of obedience or disobedience. I offer a service, I take on a job, I complete it. Once I was in the army. Special Corps. They trained me to kill and paid me a salary to do it. Then, I had to obey. Now I am my own agent. My fees are high because I'm the best.'

'When will you kill me?' she asked.

I answered with another question. 'Are you really Saint Cecilia? Is *it possible* to kill you?'

She fingered the red scar at her neck.

'I do not know. My memory comes and goes. When they found me in the street, they told me that I was. But I could only remember back a few months. I am like any believer. I doubt and then I have faith again and then I doubt. I only know that I am here for a purpose. And that when you came into the room, I recognised you. You were sent to rescue me.'

'I was sent to kill you.'

'Perhaps it is the same thing.'

I looked into her face. I knew I would have to hood that countenance if I were to earn my fee. The faces of all my victims, which must have registered in my memory though I had paid them no regard at the time, clamoured now for my attention, the double-crossers, the rivals, the inconvenient ones, all the targets that I had been paid to remove at the command of someone's vengeance or jealousy or fear or slightly founded suspicion. They swarmed across my vision, fearful, courageous, accusing, guilty, uncomprehending, unaware, as they had been at the moments of their deaths, each one steadying to meet my gaze, then swimming back into hiding in the underwater caverns of my subconscious, until they cleared and I was looking into a girl's keen eyes again.

'God will forgive you,' she said.

It was the first time she had mentioned that name.

I took the hood and pulled it over her head, securing it at the neck. It was reassuring to see her as simply a body, an object of flesh and bones and blood, her face blanked out.

She made no attempt to resist or remove the hood. She knew I was stronger than she was and would have had no trouble in subduing her but she might also have known that any resistance could have weakened my purpose. She might, at that point, have wanted death.

Do you remember the thrill, the first time that you exceeded the speed limit, the first time that you cheated at sex, the first time that you sniffed cocaine? Whatever it was that you did to break the rules, do you remember? I got that thrill every time I killed. This time, as I prepared, I was numb.

Strange memories surfaced. When I was a child – assassins have a childhood too – I had a favourite cat, hardly more than a kitten. One morning, I found it dead, its face twisted beyond recognition. During the night, death had gripped it by the throat; some feline disease had dulled its eyes and drawn a mask of mucus across them, slackened its cheeks, fixed its jaw in a terrible grimace and bared its gums. Since then I have shot cats for amusement or out of annoyance without remembering my pet. But now the dead cat's distorted features formed themselves out of the black folds of the hood like a premonition of what I would see when I lifted the material and looked at the face of dead Cecilia.

I held the gun, carefully selected for a quick, clean job, against her neck. I could see the red scar on her nape, shadowing the rim of the hood. I pulled the trigger.

The mechanism jammed.

I care for my weapons as fastidiously as a surgeon his instruments or an artist his brushes. In all my experience, a gun of mine had never malfunctioned. Now it did.

For the second time, I failed to kill Saint Cecilia.

A miraculous reprieve or simple coincidence? Whichever it was, I accepted it. I laid down the gun, loosened and removed the hood, and brought her back to the light. I tried to lessen the shock of the terrible experience she had just undergone, waiting in the darkness for the impact of a bullet that never arrived.

'It's all right,' I said. 'Nothing's going to happen. It's OK. You're safe.'

She smiled at me. 'You are my angel,' she said.

4.

Cecilia wants to disappear. She doesn't want to go back to SHIV, to the cult-overseers who had imprisoned her in a web-camera. Her mind is set on joining a band of revolutionary priests in a certain South American country. Or in her words, 'God wants me to assist them.'

I need to disappear too. My employers have been dissatisfied with my performance and I suspect they are making arrangements to recover the initial fee which they paid me. Perhaps also another assassin might be waiting with a sniper's rifle for Cecilia and me to emerge from concealment. But we do not fear that ambush any more than we quake when I see that our hiding place is about to be raided. Police marksmen are already surreptitiously taking up position outside; they think they have not been detected but I can pinpoint each of them. The high profile of this kidnapping has caught the public imagination and my protectors in the force, the long-term recipients of pay-offs, have been obliged to allow the investigation to go ahead unhindered.

We are leaving by a secret escape route I have long prepared. My bribes are still good among the security guards at the small south coast airport we will use for the first stage of our flight. Cecilia admires the device in the wall which allows us to step into a tunnel and which closes behind us seamlessly.

I carry a long gun in my right hand and a hold-all in my left, packed simply with everything we will need for our safety on this journey. The gun is not for killing. It is for guarding Saint Cecilia. She walks with an adolescent eagerness.

I am walking beside her on light feet.

It is as if she has given me wings.

Catherine Chanter
Catherine Chanter grew up in Bristol and went on to study English Literature at St. Anne's College, Oxford. She worked as a political lobbyist, both in the UK and the USA, but having become disillusioned with the process, she re-trained as a teacher. She has worked in a wide range of settings supporting children with significant emotional and behavioural difficulties. This has inspired much of her work, including programmes for Radio 4 and poetry and short stories published in anthologies by Cinnamon Press, Leaf Books and Earlyworks Press, as well as various journals.

The Boys Guide to Winning: No.1 – Hide and Seek *Shared 3rd Prize*

Catherine Chanter

It had taken a while but at last (and it really was at last) Joseph understood that hide and seek was a very complicated game because for most people the point was not only to find, but to be found. Not being found meant one of three things: either the seeker had to surrender – making you unpopular; or you had been forgotten – mummified between the dead men's suits hanging in the dark oak wardrobe; or it meant you did not want to be found – in which case, in a sense, you would have won, but then why did you play in the first place? This was one reason why Joseph was in the freezer.

Thirty

Twenty nine

In the first round of the Hide and Seek game Joseph was at a disadvantage: he was a stranger both to the game and to Luke's home. It was obvious to him that the adults had conspired to get 'the new boy' invited to the ninth-birthday party and as a child looked after by order, rather than by instinct, he could sniff out insincerity like a pawnbroker fingering a fraudulent fiver. He was aware he was the subject of some interest in the village – and not just physically. In his last school in London, everyone had been half this or one third that: no-one had been completely anything like they were here. Here, nothing ever went missing, not the pieces from the jigsaws, not the pages from the book, not the balls from the mice from the computers. Here, nobody went missing either. No one was ever sent back to where they came from. Joseph thought he would probably be the first. It was just a question of when he was found out …

Twenty eight

… just as it was inevitable he was going to be found first in this game. The birthday boy continued the countdown and the others ran shrieking through the house, hurling cushions and pulling up bedspreads like an anarchic army on a daylight raid. Joseph swung right into the dining room where a huge mirror reflected six plain chairs at a ghost's banquet, two unburned candles biding their time on a polished table, three white lilies in a glass vase and certainly nowhere to hide.

Twenty seven

Twenty six

Into the hall. Ben disguised himself behind the coats; Joseph, who often put belts around his neck, thought he could have hung quite easily from the hooks if he had thought about it first. Four pink fingers betrayed the fact that Craig had shut himself in the cupboard under the stairs but couldn't quite bring himself to close the latch; Joseph knew that he would have had no problem squatting on his own in the dark. He looked up at the green carpeted staircase. Having had enough of hiding in bedrooms in a previous life, he retreated to the kitchen…

Twenty five

Twenty four

… and under the table. He was indeed the first to be found; his bare feet, awkward ankles and bony knees protruded hopelessly under the tablecloth like detached limbs from a dismantled display in a shop window. He emerged humiliated. Unsure of what to do now he was officially out, Joseph reached up to the sink so he could pretend he was getting himself a drink if anyone came in. He could at least look found.

Twenty three

He approached round two with a little more confidence. He had spotted a door on the left of the porch which led to an unused bedroom with a bathroom. Creeping in, he smelled the not-quite-lived in, not-long-died-in smell of spare rooms used for elderly relatives. He sat on the high bed, swinging his legs and recognising the crackle of the institutional waterproof sheet under the lilac duvet, before deciding that the bath offered a better hiding place. It was absurdly dry, absurdly cold and it triggered a vivid memory. He is going swimming with his first school. His red, white and blue stripy trunks are clean and ready in a supermarket plastic bag, but the pool is drained, out of use. The rest of his class are pressing their sweaty hands and dripping noses against the giant glass window, but he is climbing, clowning down the metal steps into the empty cavern, singing the words he has overheard outside the staffroom, to the glee of the cheering audience: 'Look at me! Joseph! A fish out of water!' Breast-stroking his way through the chemical air to the deep end, his laughter feels as heavy as water and he drowns in it. Ms Nicholls' orange fingernails are hanging over the edge to pull him from the bottom of the giant blue coffin and he surfaces. Except, he thought, this bath is white and it's less like a pool and more like a slab where I lie, waiting for identification in a murder programme on telly. And, he noted as he sniffed the paler warmth in the crook of his elbow, I do not smell of chlorine.

Twenty two

Twenty one

Sinking silently, licking his dry lips with the anticipation of not being found, he listened to his heart counting down. Cupboards opened, but did not close. Skeletal coat hangers chattered and haggled in the wardrobe. Bare feet squeaked and retreated. At eye level, a quivering droplet swelled beyond the point of attachment, plummeted from the silver tap and splattered into the black plughole which was rimmed with a few thin, grim hairs. Joseph preferred showers. He liked to imagine the rushing water washing his thin black body right down the drain until anyone pulling back the curtain would say – 'Oh! Where's Joseph?'

Where is Joseph?

Twenty

Nineteen

Eighteen

He must be somewhere.

Door. Creak. Bare feet. Floor. Shriek. Door. Creak. Bare feet. Floor. Shriek. Found you.

Seventeen

So to the final round before the pizza and he was behind the sofa. It was clear that he had been forgotten, but whether he had won or lost was not so easy to work out. Like a contortionist, he had flattened his skinny eight-year-old body and slid himself into the narrow gap between the back of a large crimson sofa, the white radiator and the cream wall. Initially, his high cheekbones were pressed hard against the upholstery which puffed out dust like a dragon. He wheezed slightly and his eyes itched. His glasses magnified the swirls of the elaborate patterns embossed on the velvet until they seemed to curl and coil around his twisted neck like snakes. With some wriggling and manoeuvring he managed to turn 45 degrees so that he could breathe more easily and study a brown patch on the whitewashed ceiling which, he decided, looked like the head of the devil, or a witch's cauldron, or his first foster mother's chipped teapot. This speculation helped to take his mind off his foot, which was horribly close to the pipe feeding the gurgling radiator with a ceaseless supply of boiling water. Unless the muscles in his calves paid attention, the ankle flopped and his toes were burned. He was very hot. Trapped underneath his tummy, his arm was also starting to complain. He considered moving it, but that carried the risk of causing the sofa to shift and he didn't want to be found. Or did he? Anyway, now that the pins and needles had passed, a kind numbness had left his limbs with a mechanical life of their own. The fingers took it upon themselves to feel this way and that amongst the dust. They found postcards from long-forgotten holidays, a plastic wedding ring from a Christmas cracker, half a chocolate egg before they identified something small, cold, round and solid. Instinctively, they clasped the coin like crab claws. Finders keepers losers weepers. Was he losing or winning, if nobody found him? Slowly, he realised that this felt like winning.

Sixteen

Fifteen

Fourteen

Thirteen

The smell of being no longer looked for, the smell of warm dough and garlic bread, drifted into the room. He could imagine it. Different types of pizza with patterns of peppers to pick off, anaemic mushrooms and fluorescent pineapple like a little kid's drawing, all sliced in red cardboard boxes on that treacherous tablecloth.

Twelve

He couldn't hear anything at all. Someone must have shut the door. He imagined the four boys, standing around, white. Eating. Completely themselves. He didn't mind. He liked it behind the sofa. No-one was looking for him anymore and nobody need look after him ever again. Except Luke's mother, of course, who had 'responsibilities'; she would have to have been 'approved' for this visit; she would be shitting herself. He pursed and stretched his lips in an elasticated, exaggerated way as he repeated the shit word two or three times to himself. It was not just funny, it was quite exhilarating what it felt like when he wasn't being found.

Eleven

Ten

Where on earth is he?

I hope you're not ganging up on him, the poor thing.

Don't be silly, he can't have gone home.

We are all responsible.

But that's the whole point of hide and seek.

There's no pizza until you've found him.

Nine

The boys were kind enough when they found him, given that the pizza was going rubbery and the coke was going flat. The adults gave thin shrieks of falsified admiration, squawking and flapping like geese as he grappled out of his underworld, spluttering and branded by a row of watery blisters on his toes. And that was the moment Joseph understood that for most people, the purpose of hide and seek was not only to find but to be found, but that for him, the sensation of being found was not half as good as the possibility of remaining forever hidden. And on that basis, he had just identified the perfect game to play on that most bottomless of all days in the year, his own birthday. There was to be no contact – again. His mother had perfected the art of hiding rather than seeking a long time ago.

'Just like we did at your house, Luke,' he flattered a few weeks later, gathering around him the same four boys who had been given the King's Shilling to attend his party by the caring sharing adults. 'Hide and Seek!'

Eight

Like his predecessor, Joseph had made the most of the advantage of playing at home by researching the best hiding places. So, following his game plan, he left through the kitchen door, past the pale, defrosting burgers lying like snow-encrusted cowpats on a green tray and sticking his finger in the lurid football cake which reminded him of his name and his age – as if someone thought he might have forgotten them. He tiptoed across the damp decking in his grey socks, crossed the lawn only treading on the grey crazy paving stones, never on the cracks and squeezed behind the shed, onto the rough concrete by the back gate where no-longer-needed things were dumped until someone found them a home. A cracked plastic farmyard. Two black bin liners of left-behind clothes. A freezer.

Seven

He lifted the lid and held it open, as if separating the jaws of a beached, bleached whale. Like the bath only better, whiter, cleaner, harder. *Six* There were three green peas in the corner at the bottom and the boy and the peas stared at each other, contesting ownership, as if something so small as a pea could stop him doing something so big. Joseph had to let the smooth, white lid rest on his curly, black hair whilst he wriggled his stomach onto the edge and swung one leg, then the other over the front of the freezer. *Five.* Inside, the socks seemed absurd, so struggling slightly with one hand holding the lid, he peeled them off and dropped them over the edge into the nettles, then played his toes on the damp flatness of the bottom of the freezer, like a concert pianist before his final performance flexes his fingers at the ivory keyboard. He even tried picking up one pea between his big toe and the next, but his flesh felt clumsy and unnecessary and he gave up. Now his socks were off, his jeans felt all wrong, so they went too along with the Number 9 tee-shirt he had for his birthday and his Union Jack pants. *Four* He crouched slowly, the rays from the low spring sun reducing in precise diminishing angles as he lowered the lid. *Three.* First he could hear them. Then he could not. *Two.* The jaws shut tight, sucking out the last atoms of air and shutting out the last particles of light, swallowing him whole. *One.*

The white freezer was exactly five foot and the black boy was exactly four foot seven (or four foot five, depending on whether he rested the ruler lightly on the top of his hair, or pushed it flat). He did not close his eyes. A slow, gentle, rising mist softened the lenses of his glasses, kissing the blackness and he felt no instinct to wipe away these teardrops of condensation.

Zero

Stretching out, Joseph let his head go right back. How many times in your life do you lie with your head right back, like that, on a hard flat surface, without a pillow? His stomach was taut, flattening the uprising butterflies inside. One hand reached for the unexpectedly strong, biological beat of his pulse, exposed by the reach of his arching neck. The other hand stroked the straight sides around him, containing him perfectly, holding him.

Ready or not.

Was the garden out of bounds? Was he cheating? He wondered where the rest of them had hidden.

Here I come.

If one of them was under his bed, they would be laughing with the waterproof sheet.

Soon they would be calling. We give up. We give up.

I give up. He was very happy. He had worked out how to win at Hide and Seek. Which was one reason why he was in the freezer.

Anthony Howcroft

Anthony has a Diploma in Creative Writing from Oxford University and has been published in a variety of magazines including *Succour*, *Pestle*, *The London Magazine*, and *Trespass*. His short stories have appeared in anthologies by Leaf and Invisible Ink, and his work has been broadcast on BBC Radio following a prize-winning place in the short story competition at Wells Festival of Literature. He is a Director at a major technology vendor, and spends too much time waiting around at airports. He has written two terrible novels and destroyed both.

The Cobblestones Sparkle   *Shared 3rd Prize*

Anthony Howcroft

Wednesday, nearly midnight.

The ground is thirty or forty metres below me. Maybe it's sixty metres, I'm not very good at judging heights. In fact, I'm not very good at judging lots of things. Like how much alcohol I can drink and not do something stupid. I'm balanced on the edge of a very slippery roof. The temperature is below freezing, and I'm only wearing a tee-shirt and jeans. My shirt and jacket are knotted together as a rope, and Jani is swinging this towards me. The jacket's a fake Hugo Boss I bought at the market. I don't think the stitches are very strong. I grab the end of it and the makeshift rope is stretched between us. Jani shouts, 'I can hold you.'

Jani hates me. He wants me dead. He has already punched me twice tonight, and led me into this terrifying spot. It's his idea that I swing over the huge drop to a ledge only a few centimetres wide. There is a tree underneath but if I miss that it's all cobblestones. Jani might let go of the jacket-rope, even if it doesn't break. Nobody is watching us and nobody would know. I couldn't blame him. He's my best friend.

Four hours earlier.

I get a call from Jani. He's bored and wants to hit the town. I tell him I'm strapped for cash and he says he'll lend me some until Friday. It's too cold I say, and he sulks.

'Besides,' I add, 'I'm tired.'

'From killing chickens all day?'

That's what I do for a job. It's not actually me that kills them. I collect the scraps and incinerate those bits that even the dogs won't eat. You get used to the smell. I've got an early start tomorrow, first shift. I don't want to go out. He says that Elena might join us with some of her friends.

An hour later we're walking into town. We walk fast because it's cold. It will freeze tonight, for sure. We go to a bar hidden in a corner of the medieval city walls. It's a beautiful place, really secluded and only the locals know it so you don't have to wade through tourists to get a drink. Not that there are many tourists at this time of year. The building itself is really old and the timbers are black. People must have been much smaller in the past because I'm always hitting my head on the low beams. Tonight I walk in very carefully and stay stooped. They have a special hot toddy, which is strong as an onion, and Jani orders two. 'Let's sit outside,' he says. He's always been a bit crazy.

In summer the gardens are amazing. Crammed full of laughter and conversation, a young crowd with a buzz. There are three gardens squashed around different sides of the building. Tonight, it's absolutely deserted apart from us and an acoustic guitarist. He's employed for the price of free drinks to entice trade on a week night. All three of us huddle around a brazier that could do with a few more coals. The guitar man plays a slow version of 'Riders on the Storm'.

'This is going to be a good year,' Jani says.

'It's nearly over.'

'Not for me. I always rate years from September to September.'

'We're not at school anymore.'

'It's not that. Fall is when the year really turns, isn't it?'

'When everything dies.'

'Nothing dies. The trees shed the old stuff, the rubbish. They think. Then they begin growing. You can't see it until the spring but it's happening.'

Jani is a dreamer. He always seems to have different ideas to the rest of us. Most of the time they come to nothing, but I enjoy hearing them. He is a touch under two metres tall, same as me, but slightly more solid. He has a round face like a hamster, which is covered in stubble because he hates shaving. That's what he says, anyway. I think he wants to look like Brad Pitt. I borrow some cash from him and get the next drinks so I can warm up inside the bar. I smack my head on one of the low beams and spill most of my toddy on the way out. Elena has arrived, on her own.

'Hey,' we air kiss on both cheeks.

She sits on Jani's lap. She's not that light and Jani shifts his legs to distribute her weight. Elena is always so cheerful. I think she has the prettiest face of any of Jani's girlfriends and a lovely smile, Hollywood teeth. 'How's the writing?' she asks me.

'What writing?' says Jani.

'The poetry. You are looking at the next Hora.' She gives me one of her special smiles.

'Well, I've not done as much as I'd like lately, you know…work…'

'You should. You must.' She turns to Jani. 'He's good.'

'I've never heard any. When did you hear his poetry?'

Half of me is feeling awkward. The other half feels good.

She closes her eyes. 'Entwined in silk, your hand might wave languorously, above the drenched walls of Troy…'

'When did you do that?' Jani is looking to me for the answer.

'I'm not sure, maybe the party at your apartment.'

'No,' she says, eyes still closed. 'Don't you remember?'

I put my drink down and rub my hands to keep them warm. The glass is empty. Jani shifts Elena off his lap and slides towards me along the bench. 'Don't you remember?' he mimics her. 'I remember,' I say. 'I bet you do!'

He punches me in the shoulder, playfully. Or at least, I think it was playfully. It makes my arm go numb, but I laugh as though it's all a big joke. 'You're jealous,' she says to Jani, as though shocked, then repeats it with a knowing tone. She squeezes his hamster cheeks and bends over to kiss him. I get a view of her arse. Those jeans are tight.

Elena can't stay. Early start for work, she explains. She blows me a kiss as she vanishes around the corner.

'My bladder has shrunk to the size of a pea,' I say and wander off to relieve the tension.

When I get back Jani has gone. I assume he has left to follow Elena. The guitar man nods his head towards the other garden, and continues his version of some Stones classic. I find Jani tucked in the corner, with the city walls towering behind him.

'Ko-ko-ko,' he says. That's one of his favourite jokes. 'Over here chicken-boy. I could smell you anywhere.' You would have said cluck. And cock-a-poodle-poo. I can talk about chickens in any language.

I think about calling it a night, but I see he has collected two beers. He hands me one.

'So you and Elena?' he smiles ironically.

'What do you mean?'

He takes a slug of beer and wipes the moustache off before answering.

'Do you trust me?' he asks.

'With what?'

'Either you trust someone or you don't.'

'It depends. Everything is about the situation.' He doesn't look convinced, so I go on. 'I trust my doctor. I'd let him prescribe some drugs to get rid of a cough, but I wouldn't let him perform brain surgery on me.'

'You're getting trust and responsibility mixed up. Being held accountable for your job is one thing. If you don't clean up the chicken shit you get fired.'

'That last bit's true.'

'You see, trust is blind faith. It's letting me do your brain surgery.'

'No, that's madness. I wouldn't let you near me with a scalpel.'

'Trust is madness. It's about being irrational. People aren't machines who only do things out of self-interest.'

'Aren't they?'

'Do you think people would do whatever they wanted if they thought they could get away with it?'

'Probably.'

'We're better than that.'

Jani stands up and necks his drink. 'I'll show you,' he says.

He turns his back and places one foot carefully on the wall that runs parallel to the building. His other foot he places on the opposing wall, so he straddles both and is nestled deep in the right-angled corner. The stones are large but rough and he grabs two handholds at head height.

Then he says, 'Follow me.'

Next thing he begins springing up the wall. Not really climbing, he uses his legs in a rigid way, locking them out and then pushing up in a mini-jump. He scales the wall at a frightening pace. I shout and he yells in exhilaration. I have to take a few paces back to watch properly. His right foot is on the old city structure, but the left wall is formed by stones from the high bell tower of a church. Like a spider pulling himself up a thread he makes jerky movements and then soars, as though he's attached to the bell tower. My breath comes out in silver clouds as I tilt my head back. At the top of the city wall, which is still some fifteen or twenty metres below the peak of the bell tower, he clambers on to the walkway and turns to wave. 'Come on up,' he shouts. 'You've always wanted to.'

I have never had any desire to climb the walls, although Jani has often talked about it on drunken summer evenings.

'The view's magnificent.' 'I'm staying down here.'

'Oh no you're not,' he says and dangles something in the air. It's small and black but I can't work out what it is at first, then I have a sinking feeling. My wallet.

'Bastard!'

I plant a foot on each wall and try to copy his technique for bouncing up. It's much easier than I thought. In fact, it's so easy that I quite enjoy it. When I get about three quarters of the way up I suddenly realize how high I've come, and how easily I could plummet. My legs begin to shake and my tongue sticks to my mouth as though I've been drinking glue. I stop.

'Keep moving,' Jani says.

I struggle for the last few feet and he yanks my hand and pulls me on to the ledge. We look over the battlements, those seesaw bits. I forget the word. The city is laid out for us, sparkling in the perfect cold air. Jani says it looks like a treasure chest that's been kicked over, spilling jewels across the ground. I think it looks like one of those photos of another galaxy where each tiny dot is another sun and you feel really small and insignificant.

I turn to say something and find Jani walking along the ledge, heading into the old town, passing the tower and wandering the walls' zigzag route that reveals the original boundary. I shuffle behind him, keeping a tight hold of the wall. He stops on top of a small supporting buttress, with a square area of a few feet where we can both stand. Unlike the tourist sections of the wall, this has no handrails.

'Hit me,' he says and pats his stomach.

'Haven't we done enough tonight?'

'Go on,' he says. 'Hard. I'm ready.' He braces.

You never want to hit too hard. There was Houdini's death for one thing, plus the fact that your opponent gets to hit you back. That's our rule. Going first is worst, calculating how hard to hit. I feel strangely liberated though. He's near the edge, but if he falls off it will be his own fault.

I swing hard. He swivels, which isn't allowed. You have to stand still and take it. I miss and stagger forward. I nearly choke on my heart, it leaps so high. I'm going to fall off. Jani grabs me before I topple. He laughs. I swear, in shock first, then anger.

'Hit me,' he says again. 'Give it all you've got.'

This time the wall is behind him, and I don't wait for a second request. I catch him hard. He sinks back against the stones and doubles up.

'Are you OK?' I ask. He shakes his head and lets out a partial laugh.

'Good one,' he coughs then asks, 'my turn?'

I can't say no. We switch positions. I wait with the wall behind me. He hits hard, but with less venom than I did. I double over to mirror his actions, so he thinks the punches are equal. Otherwise he'll try harder next time.

When I've regained control I remember why I climbed the walls.

'My wallet,' I say.

'Here it is.'

He holds it in front of me and then when I reach for it he pulls his hand back. I lunge forward, the effect of which is simply to knock the wallet out of his hand. There's a flat roof not so far away, at about the same height as us. The wallet lands there and slides. I think for a moment it might go right over the other side but it stops not far beyond the middle.

'We can get that,' says Jani. There's some restoration work taking place on the next section of wall, and Jani goes to collect a plank and pushes it out to form a bridge to the roof.

'I'll hold this end,' he says.

'I'm not walking over there. You're the one that caused all this. You can go.'

'It's not my wallet.'

'Shit.'

It's a long drop, but there's a tree beneath. I tell myself any fall will be broken, and the worst I'll get are some scratches.

'Put all your weight on it.' I say.

He kneels down on one end of the plank and ducks his head since I have to step over him to get on. I keep hold of the wall to steady myself at first, then turn around and spread my arms out like a tightrope walker.

'Don't look down.' Jani says.

'How am I meant to see the plank?'

I start slowly and get faster. The plank is bouncy and it gets worse the further along I go, so I walk quicker and quicker, jumping the last section to land on the roof. Thank God it doesn't give way. Jani cheers, and cautiously I move out to the centre, prodding the roof with the tip of my sneakers, hoping it's solid. I pick up the wallet and then hear Jani swear. A second or two later there's a crash far below.

Jani is still on the wall, looking at me. 'The plank fell off,' he says.

'Get another.'

'It was the only one.'

I walk towards the edge and we stare at each other.

'It's not that far,' he says.

'Oh no.'

'If you ran from the other side of the roof, you could easily make it.'

'No way.'

'You were good at the long jump. Didn't you break a record in year eight?'

'I'm not doing it.'

There's silence. We stand only a few feet apart, but are separated by a dark space that could suck either of us into it like a black hole.

'What's in the wallet?' he asks.

'Hey?'

'You said you were out of cash, so what's in the wallet that's so valuable?'

'The usual. Credit cards and stuff.'

'You haven't got a credit card.'

The alcohol is wearing off, and I begin to remember how cold it is. How cold I am. My fingers are going numb, my legs stiffening up.

'Take off your shirt and jacket,' Jani says.

'What?'

'We can make a rope.'

'No way.'

'Ko-ko-ko!' he flaps some imaginary wings.

The rope doesn't sound such a bad idea, and I don't have any others. I make the best knots I know how and pull them incredibly hard to make sure they are tight. Then I throw the whole thing to Jani, since it's not quite long enough to reach, and he ties his jacket on to make it longer. Then he swings it out to me a few times until I grasp hold of it. I'm standing right on the edge, which is icy, and very slippery. The cobblestones sparkle like stars, or perhaps diamonds. 'I can hold you,' Jani shouts.

'About Elena…'

'Jump.'

Given everything that has happened recently, or even just tonight, I shouldn't rely on Jani. He's angry. He's drunk. He knows more than he says. Yet as he said earlier, trust is irrational. Life would be hell without some people you can always count on. I jump.

Swinging like Tarzan, I hit the wall hard. I don't let go, and the stitches don't break, immediately. I dangle. Looking up, I see Jani straining to hold me. I can hear tiny ripping noises. 'Use your legs,' he says, 'push.'

I scramble and push. He pulls but mostly he holds on, keeping his weight anchored and low so we don't topple to the cobblestones together. I get one hand over the edge and then another. He loops the rope over part of the wall's battlements and grabs my hands to help me roll on to the walkway. Relief floods through me. We sit back to back and listen to our breathing. I'm not so cold anymore.

'Your face is a mess.' Jani says even though he is not facing me. I touch it and realise I'm bleeding. I'm not sure if I've broken my nose or split my lip. Everything is beginning to hurt. We make our way along the wall. A quarter of a mile further there are some steps where the tourist section starts, and we walk down to street level. He wants me to go to the hospital. I go home instead.

In my room, I wash my face and check for damage. My lip is swollen but nothing seems to be broken. I take my wallet, open it and remove my picture of Elena. I screw it up and drop it in the bin.

Susan Akass

Susan Akass has been writing since the early nineties and has written a number of children's picture books, including *Number Nine Duckling* and *Grizzly Bears*. She has also written many children's readers for national and international reading schemes, her most popular character being 'Pirate Pete'. Her previous short story successes are runner-up in the first Independent/Scholastic Children's Story of the Year competition and an adult story 'The Tree', broadcast on Radio 4. She lives with her husband in Bath where she teaches full-time.

Facing Up To Things

Susan Akass

That was it then. A life over, a death over. The funeral was finished, everyone had gone home and she was on her own. It was time to face up to things, as her mother would have told her, one of the millions of pieces of advice given to her over a lifetime. And the things she had to face up to… his car, which she couldn't drive, waiting to be sold; his clothes in the wardrobe, needing to be sorted for the charity shop; his golf clubs blocking the hall, looking for a home; his side of the bed, empty.

Just now at 9.30 pm, she had to put out the milk bottle, her job. But she also had to lock up, his job. She had to fold up the newspaper and put it in the box under the stairs, her job. She also had to switch out all the lights and close the downstairs doors, his job. All their little roles, which had evolved over fifty years of marriage, now came down to her, to Valerie Wilkinson, there on her own, shifting uncomfortably from room to room, aware only of the emptiness of her house, of her life, of her future.

But that wasn't the way to think, or so her children had told her. They had told her how she must be positive. How she had still got them and her grandchildren, her friends and her health. But the boys and their wives had gone home now. Back to their own lives. They couldn't spend any more time there, with her, sorting out her life. Anyway, she realized, they were too scared to help. They had been tiptoeing around her feelings since it happened. 'Shall we move his razor from the bathroom?' she had heard them whisper together. 'Where shall we put his spectacles?' But she knew what they were feeling. The whole house was impregnated with him. Move his things and he would be gone. They couldn't face that.

But she could. She must. She decided to start there and then with a bin bag. She would just clear the surfaces. Bathroom first. The razor could go, and his spectacles, his toothbrush, all his bottles of aftershave and the magazines he read on the loo. Bedroom next. Nothing much there. If any room in the house was hers it was this one. His dressing gown hung behind the door. She would have to wash it before she put it back in the wardrobe with the rest of his clothes. She picked it up and buried her face in it, inhaling his smells. No, she wouldn't wash it yet. She picked up his book from beside the bed. She would return it to the bookcase in the study.

The study: the study was harder. She could still see him lying there, roughly covered by the blanket which the ambulance men left when they decided that there was nothing more they could do. She wanted to put the whole room in the bag. She especially wanted his computer to go, the computer where he was working when the blood vessel in his brain blew. Why had it been his brain and not the computer's? She didn't understand computers and wanted to be rid of it. But how do you get rid of a computer? She couldn't take that down to the charity shop and she wouldn't know how to start writing an ad for the local paper. Best ask one of the boys to take it, but which one? They had always been an acquisitive lot, her boys. No doubt they couldn't wait to get their hands on his stuff and, oh, how they would argue over it.

She was getting distracted. Of course she must face the study. She opened the door. She avoided looking at his ghost lying on the floor and scanned the room for contributions to her bin bag. There on the desk was the box of chocolates he had almost finished that last night. He wouldn't let her have any... 'You're getting too fat,' he said and he was right, not that he didn't have a gut on him himself.

She emptied his bin and then said loudly, breaking the silence, 'That's enough for tonight. I'm too tired.'

Tomorrow would be another day, and the next day and the next. She could foresee an endless stream of indistinguishable tomorrows.

'No! Don't be like that. Think positive.'

She would go to bed that night without a sleeping pill, she decided resolutely. She was sure that she was tired enough after 'bearing up' all day. What did those words mean? 'And how are you bearing up?' they had all asked at the funeral. 'Oh well enough,' she had replied, smiling stoically when everything inside her was groaning with the meaninglessness of it all. Yes, she would face tonight without a sleeping pill. She had used them for five nights in a row because she had needed something to make her close her eyes and forget, but she couldn't keep using them forever.

She fell asleep almost instantly; half woke later feeling cold and turned over to hug Derek. His absence shocked her back into wakeful reality. She lay in the darkness hugging herself and feeling the weight of emptiness beside her. After fifty years of sleeping with Derek, her body expected him to be there. How long before she could train it to sleep alone?

As she lay there, trying to relax her limbs and still her mind, she became aware of faint noises. Though her hearing wasn't too good these days, she was sure that she could hear the sound of movement downstairs. She tensed, listening hard for a few minutes and heard nothing more. If Derek had been there he would have got up to investigate. He often had. Off he'd go, prowling the house in his pyjamas and finding nothing. 'Better to be safe than sorry,' he would say climbing back into bed with cold feet.

She pulled the blankets tightly around her. If there had been no one there in all their years together, why should there be a burglar now.

Then a heavy crash and a man's cry of pain sounded through the house loud and clear.

What on earth was going on? She switched on the bedside light, hauled herself out of bed, pulled on her dressing gown and slippers and walked stiffly but determinedly downstairs. In the back of her head a voice was saying, 'Take care… this could be dangerous… why don't you phone the police?' but at that moment she was simply, profoundly curious.

Strange grunts were emanating from the lounge as she switched on the light. There she was confronted by a most extraordinary sight: the legs and bottom of a man, clad in tatty jeans and trainers, pinned down by the sash window. His toes just reached the floor but he couldn't get enough purchase to force the window up with his back. He was squirming like an insect under a knife. She was tempted to laugh but then realized how painful his situation must be. The rotten sash cord must have snapped as he was making his exit and the hugely heavy, Victorian sash window had fallen on him. It must have hurt terribly.

'Can I help you?' she asked and only later reflected how ridiculous this must have sounded to the burglar, trapped in her lounge window. Why hadn't she said something like, 'Got you. The police are on their way. Don't even think of trying to escape.' It was only later in her fantasies that she thought of more appropriate, crime-fiction style responses.

But no, what she said was 'Can I help you?' A grunt of reply came from outside the window. Unhesitating, she walked over, awkwardly straddled the man's legs, feeling the pain in her arthritic knees, and began to heave on the heavy sash. She hated dealing with these windows. Derek had always said that she had an attitude problem over them; she didn't believe she could open them and therefore never could. She knew it had nothing to do with attitude. She knew that she just wasn't strong enough, particularly in the winter when the rain swelled the frames.

'Just an inch or two,' the man's voice muttered 'and I might be able to squeeze back in.'

She heaved again but the window seemed to be sticking fast.

This was the moment at which she would have called Derek. Two tries and give up. Call in reinforcements. Summon some masculine help. But there was no longer any masculine help to summon. Do it yourself, she told herself. She took a deep breath and on the exhalation she heaved again. The window shifted a few inches, she stepped to one side, still holding it with all her strength, and the man wriggled back into the room. He sat back with a thump and a groan on the dark green lounge carpet.

He was older than she had expected. The papers led you to believe that most break-ins were performed by teenage yobs. This man must have been in his late twenties. His hair was cropped short, he had a row of earrings in one ear and was wearing a dirty sweat shirt. No doubt he would have tattoos up his arms and would own a large dog. She knew the type. Her generation distrusted them. Only last week one of her friends had moved house and had described her removal men, with their tattoos and piercings, in terms of horror. They would have been clones of this burglar. She knew that she too should have distrusted this man. She had every reason to. However, what concerned her now was that he was in considerable pain. What he should have done was to knock her away and run; self- preservation demanded it. Instead he was sitting there on her lounge carpet, looking white and shocked, with his hands clutching his back.

'Are you hurt? Shall I look?' She didn't give him a chance to reply but instead knelt creakily behind him and lifted his sweat shirt, as if he was one of her sons. There was an ugly, dark red bruise already forming across the small of his back and the skin was broken. She was worried about his spine. 'Can you move your legs alright?' He wiggled his feet a little and nodded. He seemed to be gritting his teeth with pain. 'I'll get you an ice pack.' She struggled to her feet by clutching the seat of the armchair and then hurried to the kitchen for a pack of frozen peas. She wrapped it carefully in a clean, pressed tea towel and returned. She placed it gently against his back where he held it. He said nothing.

'Tea?' she asked and without waiting for a response, returned to put on the kettle.

'Have you phoned the cops?' he asked in a surly voice as she sat down in an armchair waiting for the kettle to boil. She was conscious suddenly that her teeth were still in a glass in the bathroom and her grey, permed hair was in wild disarray. What must he think of her, this crazy old woman?

'No.'

'Are you going to?'

'What will you do if I do?'

'Get out.'

'I'm not going to.'

Why ever not?, she thought. She had a duty to turn him in. Old women like her got raped and beaten up by young men like him, but sitting there on the carpet, with his peas clutched to his back, he didn't look like much of a threat.

'What were you going to steal?'

'Whatever I could find …telly, computer stuff, jewellery.' His voice had changed. No longer surly, there was a hint of bravado in it. He'd lost face, now he was trying to save it again. He shrugged and winced. 'The telly's in the flower bed,' he added, 'That was what I was shifting when the window fell.'

Why hadn't she noticed it was gone? It was big enough. Derek's pride and joy. The hours he had spent watching golf on that telly. The room was much nicer without it. She had always hated it. She preferred to listen to the radio. A real Radio 4 addict, that was how Derek described her.

'Well you can have that,' she said surprising herself. 'I don't want it.'

'Come again?' he said.

'You can have the telly. I don't want it. Come to think of it you can have the computer as well and what about golf clubs? Do you want those? Her mind began to race. And there's a car on the drive. A Toyota. Quite a new one. The keys are by the front door, but then I suppose you must have a car to take away the things you were going to steal.'

'Well yeah,' he said, 'but my mate pissed off with that when he saw the light come on.'

'Well there's your answer then,' she said. 'Let's have that cup of tea and then I'll help you load it up.'

'Lady,' he said, as she returned with the mugs. 'Are you out of your mind?'
'No, very much in it,' she replied smiling. 'I'm just facing up to things.'

———

'And you heard nothing at all,' the kindly police lady asked the next morning.
'No nothing,' replied Valerie. 'You see I'd taken a sleeping pill. I can't sleep
since my husband passed away. It was a terrible shock when I woke to find
everything gone.'

'All Dad's stuff,' murmured her eldest son, who had rushed round to support
her in this latest hour of need.

'All Dad's stuff,' she reiterated solemnly.

Irene Black

Irene Black's short stories, articles and poems have won prizes, including first prize in the 2003 National Association of Writers Groups annual short story competition. She has been a published short story prizewinner in *Writers' News* and *Writers' Forum*. Her novels, *The Moon's Complexion* (2005) and *Darshan* (2008), both set partly in India, are published by Goldenford Publishers Ltd, a company she helped to found in 2004. *The Moon's Complexion* is also published electronically by American publisher Virtual Tales. She holds an MA in Indian Temple Architecture and draws upon her research in some of her books and short stories.

The Loi Krathong

Irene Black

Dao sat hunched up in the doorway of the photographer's shop behind her father's noodle stall, hiding her despair beneath the curtain of her covering hands. Dawn was breaking but to her it felt like twilight.

She had, in her father's eyes, brought shame upon him. In his eyes, she had deserved her punishment. The wheals on her bare arms throbbed and reddened. Beneath the angry imprint of her father's fist upon her cheek the blood surged and the flesh swelled.

But Dao did not bemoan the pain, or even the shame. It was her father's shame, not hers. Dao grieved for the death of the future that she had dreamt about so often; the future that gave meaning to her life.

She loved her father and hadn't wanted to hurt him. Her mother had died many years ago. Her brother Yai had gone. Only Dao and her father remained to set up the noodle stall every morning in front of the photographer's shop, where they rented two small rooms on the top floor.

The photographer, Chai Son, had been at school with Yai and despite their differing fortunes, he had become good friends with Dao's father. Since the requirement for passport photographs had infiltrated so many aspects of Thai life, Chai Son had become one of the most successful businessmen in the area. The noodle stall, however, despite its popularity, provided only a modest livelihood, as Dao's father kept the prices low to allow the poor as well as the rich to indulge their taste buds.

Now, because of Dao, the friendship between Chai Son and her father was shattered. Never again would Chai Son be welcome at their stall, and they would probably have to find somewhere else to live.

For Chai Son, with the most innocent of intentions, had compromised Dao's father's honour.

'I heard you weeping last night, Dao. Why so sad?' Chai Son had asked her as she set out for school the previous day.

'My father says I cannot graduate from high school,' she told him. 'From tomorrow I must stay at home and work at the noodle stall.'

She had greeted her father's decision with disbelief. Yai had been allowed to graduate so Dao had automatically assumed that she would do the same. Yai had gone on to Chulalongkorn University – the most prestigious in Thailand. A poster-sized photograph of him receiving his degree from their beloved king was proudly displayed on the stall. Now Yai was a busy university lecturer, who rarely had time to visit them.

'How long until you should graduate?' Chai Son said.

'Two years, Khun Chai Son.'

'It is possible to do this at night school.'

'Yes, Khun Chai Son, but the fees are beyond our means.'

'But not beyond mine. I will sponsor you. During the day you can work for your father. At night you can go to school.'

'Khun Chai Son, I could not repay you. And my father would never agree.'

'I will talk to him. As for repayment, you and your father have repaid me a thousand times simply by your friendship.'

Dao could hardly believe her good fortune. She ran to the bus stop, her mind filled with thoughts of study and success – even the possibility of university.

When she got home after school, her father was waiting for her upstairs. He steadied himself against the wall. A can of beer was clutched so tightly in his hand that froth seeped out and trickled onto the wooden floorboards.

'How dare you ask help from Chai Son,' he roared. 'We take charity from no one. You have dishonoured the name of our family. You have brought shame upon our ancestors.'

Then he had beaten her, but the lashes from his tongue had caused her the greater pain.

Night brought no comfort. She dreamt that she was a white-feathered hen, senseless with fear, trussed upside-down with a dozen others on the back of a motorcycle heading to the meat market.

Near the doorway where Dao was sitting, a loudspeaker sprang into life. Through her misery, she became aware of music; a popular song played every year only on this day. *Loi Krathong, Loi Krathong,* came the refrain. She shook herself from her stupor as she remembered that this evening the most beautiful of all Thai festivals would take place.

In front of her on the pavement Dao's father had set up little plastic stools for his customers, and had opened up the noodle stall. A massive pot of steaming broth sizzled on the charcoal stove, sending out aromas to tempt even the most determined dieter. Metal dishes overflowed with rice noodles of various shapes and sizes, shrimps, oysters, little crabs, Chinese parsley, coriander; scallions, lemon grass, lime.

Despite the early hour a few customers were already assembled and Dao's father was busy. He had not called upon Dao to help. She knew he was biding his time, allowing space between his anger and her despair. Later she would be expected to slip in unobtrusively to take her turn at the stall.

She stood up and drawing her thick, black hair across her injured cheek, ambled out into the sticky heat of the city.

Everywhere stalls were setting up. The stallholders greeted her with a smile or a cheery wave, but she hardly acknowledged them; the charcoal chicken seller, the kebab and sausage vendor, the old woman selling deep-fried bananas who followed Dao's progress with a puzzled expression – never before had Dao passed by her stall in the morning without purchasing a bagful of her crisp, delicious banana snacks.

Today the number of stalls had been boosted by the influx of temporary carts and tables packed with plate-sized boats, *krathongs,* in the form of lotus flowers. This evening under the full moon they would be launched onto the river to honour the water goddess, Mae Khongka, and to pay homage to the footprint of the Buddha. The variety of *krathongs* was endless. Traditional ones were created on a base of banana stem, but these days they were more often built on a round piece of stiff polystyrene. Some were decorated with real banana leaves and flowers, others with paper ones. All were adorned with incense sticks, a little flag and a candle to light them on their way. Some were made out of pastry, to become food for the fish rather than pollution for the river.

Suddenly longing overwhelmed her. If only she could be one of those *krathongs* floating to oblivion in the arms of the water goddess.

As she reached the end of the street and stood watching the wide river, the idea possessed her mind like roots of a great bo-tree enveloping the ruins of an ancient temple. Out there, beyond the reach of man, where the river became one with the great ocean – out there was peace. No noodle stall, no beatings, no yearning for what could not be.

Yes, she would do it. At midnight when the celebrations died down and the noodle stall had served its last customer, she would slip down to the temple by the river. She would ask Lord Buddha for his blessing and light the candle on her own *krathong*. Then she would descend the temple steps to the river, and surrender herself to the warm, swirling waters. The current would carry her away from the bank and when the wind blew out the candle on her *krathong*, it would blow away her memories, her desires and her sorrow.

In the morning when they cleared the debris from the river, they would find her *krathong*. They would know it was hers because it would be the most beautiful of all. It would be her message to the world, her suicide note. *In life I could not achieve my dreams but in death I am free and will blossom like the lotus flower and shine like candlelight.*

She stood for a moment in silence, the first silence she had known for two days. Like a ship, whose engines have stopped, at peace. Then she turned away and headed home.

On her way back to the noodle stall, Dao called in at the supermarket and selected a polystyrene *krathong* base, the largest she could find. She bought joss sticks, a little saffron flag and the finest candle in the shop, creamy-pink and fat, with a good, strong wick.

Next she stopped at a flower stall. She spent some minutes sifting through the mounds of flora and foliage. Finally she picked out a fresh banana leaf, a coconut palm frond, ten orange marigolds, five white roses, and two-dozen purple orchids.

Settled once more in Chai Son's doorway, Dao worked on her *krathong*. From the banana leaf she formed petals, fixing them to the base until it resembled a green lotus blossom. Then she decorated it with the remaining leaves and flowers. Finally she secured the flag, the joss sticks and the candle into the centre. All the time she worked she felt nothing but an overwhelming sense of harmony. When her *krathong* was finished she held it at arm's length. It was indeed a work of art, a fitting coda to her dance of life.

Dao stood up and placed the *krathong* carefully on a stool next to the noodle stall, where she could keep an eye on it while she worked. Then she took her place behind the cooking pot and eased the soup ladle out of her father's hand. Briefly he caught her eye, nodded and slipped away. Mechanically Dao took over the task of cooking, serving, taking payment, giving change, making small talk about the coming festivities.

'That's a fine *krathong*. How much are you asking?' said a customer.

Dao shook her head.' It's not for sale.'

Moments later a stranger stopped by. 'A hundred *baht* for that *krathong*,' he said.

Again Dao shook her head. 'Not for sale.'

Throughout the day people stopped to admire the *krathong*, declared it the finest on the street, begged Dao to sell it. But she only shook her head. 'It's not for sale.'

By the afternoon the street was crowded with early revellers. Now both Dao and her father worked side by side at the noodle stall, each keeping up an outward semblance of normality, the barrier between them invisible to their customers.

At five o'clock the sun began to fade and by six the sky was dark but the street was bright with shop lights and the fires from the roadside stoves. The crowds were intense. People picked their way from one stall to the next, sampling the festival delicacies at each; a *roti* here, a crisp pancake there, a bag of deep-fried grubs, a barbequed corncob, some crunchy locusts. Then at last the noodle-stall. Despite the many snacks already taken the communal appetite for noodles was as unremitting as ever. Dao and her father worked non-stop. At seven the floats came past but Dao hardly noticed the pretty *Loi Krathong* princesses on their lotus blossom thrones, or the clowns and the dancers and the fairy lights. She did not hear the crashing of the great side drums as the bands marched past, or the tubas and accordions, the trumpets and the flutes. She had hardly even registered Chai Son, as chief sponsor of the festival, marching at the head of the whole procession. She crossed the turbulent skies of celebration on autopilot, waiting for the moment when she could switch to manual landing.

Across the road a dais had been set up and an official with a microphone requested Khun Chai Son to honour the proceedings by accepting a special *krathong* with which to open the ceremony.

Chai Son stepped up onto the dais. The official eulogized about the super-splendid, super-sized *krathong*, especially imported for Khun Chai Son from the USA. Dao's father sneered.

Chai Son waited. The official waited. A helper hurried across and whispered in the official's ear. The official looked aghast.

'Ahem,' he said finally, 'forgive the delay. It seems the *krathong* has been misplaced.'

Chai Son waited. The official stared at his feet. The crowds muttered. The helpers ran around like frightened rabbits.

For the first time Dao paid attention to the day's events. Chai Son's embarrassment had rekindled a flicker of feeling in her heart. She had no time to think. What she had to do was clear. She picked up her *krathong* and walked across to the dais.

'Not misplaced,' she said, handing it to him, 'not misplaced at all.' Before he had time to respond, she turned and walked back to the noodle stall. Her father was looking across at Chai Son. There was pride on his face and the glimmer of a smile. Chai Son held up the *krathong* and nodded at Dao's father. Honour had been restored.

Harmony returned to Dao's heart. Now she would leave behind no discord to linger in those she loved. She shrugged off the loss of the *krathong*. She had no need for earthly symbols. No words would be inscribed upon her watery tomb. She would leave no epitaph except the empty space where she once stood.

By the approach of midnight many of the stalls were shutting down, the shop lights were extinguished and most of the *krathongs* had been sent on their way downstream, little boats of flickering light in the black water. With each one had gone a secret prayer, a wish, a hope.

It was time.

'Father. I have not yet launched a *krathong*. May I go now before the day ends?'

Dao's father nodded briefly. 'Go. I will finish here.'

Dao slipped up to her room above Chai Son's shop. She took off her grease-stained clothes and put on a red silk sarong and her best white blouse of crocheted flowers. Then she made her way barefoot in the darkness to the riverside temple. She knelt before the golden Buddha image, brought her hands together and bent to touch her forehead to the ground. For a few moments she knelt silently, clearing her mind of its final earthly thoughts. Then she stood up and walked out of the temple onto the steps leading down to the water.

She carried on walking, not pausing when the last step ended and the water began. The river was deep and she felt the warm flow dragging her down.

Then a strong hand gripped her arm and a force greater than the current lifted her. She let out a cry of happiness. The water goddess was taking her home. Peace and joyful surrender penetrated every facet of her being.

'Open your eyes, Dao. Come on. Open your eyes.' Not the water goddess, but a man's voice, a familiar voice. Confusion gripped her. She was being wrenched back out of her state of bliss. Beneath her was a hard surface. She was no longer in the river. She started to scream and thrash about. Someone was shaking her. She felt the water goddess gush from her lungs and out of her mouth. Then she opened her eyes.

'Chai Son,' she gasped.

'Now you will be all right,' came Chai Son's gentle voice.

For a few moments Dao sat propped up against a wall, shivering more from grief and shock than cold. Chai Son crouched by her side, brushing the hair off her face and stroking her arms.

Finally Dao felt reality returning and could grasp what had happened. Anger overwhelmed her.

'Why did you stop me, Chai Son?'

'I knew,' he replied. 'I knew from the look on your face when you gave me the *krathong*. You had given up on the world.'

'Why did you stop me? You had no right'

'Is the world such a hostile place for you, Dao? Is there nothing to keep you here? Not your father? Or your brother? Not your future?'

'Future? There is no future for me. My destiny is to live my life as a chattel. I was so very nearly free and content. Now you have cast me back into this life of slavery. Is that what you wish for me?'

'There is another way, Dao, and the answer lies within you.'

'How can that be? Night school is forbidden me. Nothing else matters.'

'Night school is not forbidden you. Only the fees. I cannot help you, but you can help yourself.'

'How?'

'Today you showed the world that you are a fine artist. Your hands can mould flowers in a way others only dream of. You could have sold that *kraihong* a thousand times at unheard of prices.'

'So?'

'So you can earn enough to pay your own way through night school. And still help your father on the stall.'

'Khun Chai Son, have you forgotten that *Loi Kraihong* is only once a year? How do I earn my fees on the other three hundred and sixty-four days?'

'Temple gods need garlands, Dao. House gods also. Road vehicles wear flower offerings to bless their journeys. Many festivals are held throughout the year. You have a great gift, Dao. Use it to make your dreams come true.'

'You make it sound so easy,' Dao murmured, 'but I am so alone.'

'No, Dao,' Chai Son said slowly. 'You are not alone. Never alone.' Dao could not answer but when she looked into Chai Son's tender eyes there were tears in her own.

'If you believe in me,' she whispered, then nothing is impossible.'

Chai Son pressed her hand. 'Come,' he said, 'Let us go home now.'

Sue Coffey

Sue Coffey is from the Cynon Valley and now lives in Cardiff. She also lived Cyprus for many years. Sue, who has an MA in Creative Writing, works for a training association and moonlights as a Tutor on the Learn programme at Cardiff University. Her short stories have been published in national magazines and Honno anthologies. She has won two South and Mid Wales Association of Writers awards and her work has been long-listed for a Cinnamon Press Award and short-listed for the Legend Writing Award both in 2007. She is currently working on a collection of stories.

Hunters and Gatherers

Sue Coffey

There are those who say it was the winter wind betrayed our presence. And it's true it howled around the mountains that bitter solstice like a woman in childbirth or mourning. It's as good a reason as any. And we, who weave our history for those who follow, must tell of how the Hunters came and what befell. My travail is almost upon me. I am unused to idleness. It seems wrong to do no more than feed and stir a pot while others labour from dawn to dusk in the fields. This then will be my appointed task: to use the rising steam and smoke as if it were wool for carding. From these swirling wisps I will tease out possibility and spin words to clothe the legend.

I call silently for strength before I bow my head, gently rocking and crooning as if at a Gathering. I breathe deeply and narrow my eyes as if against the glare of snow as the vision sharpens. 'They appeared,' it will be said, 'from where mist meets cloud.'

Now the chill of that other day penetrates my fur cloak as I watch ten horsemen emerge from the narrow pass. They bang flakes from blanketed shoulders and rein in weary horses. Desperate eyes scan the icy hills. But there is no sign of the nimble-footed beast that has lured them to this bleak place with promises of feast as hollow as their grumbling bellies. One and all, they sag back in the saddle like under-filled sacks of wheat. The raw wind robs them of breath and speech. Let the next snowfall bury them: they can go no further. Then the

57

one we knew later as Wulfstan raises his head. His falcon-nose sniffs in disbelief. Madness, in the middle of this *nothingness*, but there it is again – a shred of roasting meat, hooked on the teeth of the gale. And something else impossible which they all hear: a whisper of pipes and bells. Chapped grins split their hoar-frosted beards. Who would have thought it – spoils of war at the arse-end of this God forsaken country.

Slithering and cursing, they navigate the sloping valley sides wondering at the lack of a worn track. But they follow their leader unhesitatingly. It is his wits that have kept them one ride ahead of the gallows' long shadow.

Our old shepherd, simple-minded and mute, is the first to die. He sees them as they leave the shelter of the broad-leafed wood for the pasture where he tends the sheep in clement weather and where he is drawn this day by habit. Too foolish to run for his life he is left in their wake, his head cleft with an axe. When the Hunters reach our settlement it puzzles them. What fools are these: no defensive wall or stockade and no-one looking out to warn of enemies? Under the darkening sky they spur their horses on.

I move restlessly and sigh as bodily pain reminds me of other hurts. We were happy that day in the Great Hall, putting the preparations for celebration in place. The tables were piled with swathes of winter berries and evergreen leaves when the door crashed open. They swept in, demons from a nightmare, trampling clean rushes with filthy boots.

Our young musicians, boys with hairless chins, were cut down before they could move, as was the hound that leapt to our defence. Then there was near silence as our screams faded to whimpering and trembling. The loudest sound was the panting of the trespassers as they surveyed their spoils, wiping scarlet blades on deer-skin sleeves. The mother of the new girl-child, who moments before had giggled and tested out the place of honour, now hugged the babe to her, muffling the weak keening lest it invite swift retribution.

'Where are your weaponed-ones?' The Hunters demanded, glaring around. 'Tell us!'

'If you please, Sir.' Instinct led me to address the tall young man who stood apart with an air of authority.

Wulfstan nodded his permission for me to speak.

'We have not seen our protectors since they left for the war, a long time ago. You will find no swords or spears here, only spindles.'

He pointed at the new mother and baby. 'Then how came she by that? Witchcraft?'

His men laughed coarsely. I looked to where the eldest of the dead lay beneath his lyre. 'He cannot harm you now.' 'And who are you?' Wulfstan asked. 'That you speak for all?'

'Edyth,' I said. 'Wife of Aelfric, church elder.'

'Or widow.' He appraised my comely face and form. It was as if he were running a hot, hard hand over the skin beneath my shift. 'Your lord is a long time gone, you say.'

'Don't believe the elf-shot,' someone yelled. 'They cannot be alone here. The men have seen us and are hiding in the hills.'

Wulfstan took a stride toward me and wrenched up my chin to better search my face as he spoke. 'Does the wife of Aelfric know Canute's Law? What treatment befits a woman guilty of adultery?'

I knew: none better. The answer caught in my throat like a fishbone as I stammered. 'Her husband will have her property and she will lose her nose and ears...'

'If you have lied to us, to me, you will *beg* for so lenient a punishment.'

I was pushed away. 'Bring us food: good meat, bread, ale. The best you have.'

We had no choice but to bring out our hoarded foodstuffs and watch as they devoured it. As the evening wore on we tried to shrink from their calculating glances and clutching hands but soldiers are soldiers, even bedraggled ones. We saw it in their eyes. They intended to rut with us like animals in the field once they had satisfied other appetites. We would not be able to gainsay them. Even as they became louder and drunker they kept men posted to watch for the men-folk they suspected would make a counter attack. Their weapons were always ready at arms-reach.

But our eyes did not alight with hope on the doors or our ears strain for the sound of salvation. Our faith lay elsewhere: in our ability to overcome and survive.

My, but they were ravenous, calling for pot after pot of our stew. They ate until their stomachs were distended and their knives had polished the clay bowls clean. Then they set about scratching other itches. One by one they stumbled out into the freezing night, dragging their chosen women with them to hunt for beds. I guessed then that it would be but the first of many such nights.

Wulfstan did not trouble himself with finding a comfortable pallet. He raped me on the hearth by the light of the dying embers. He was rough and quick as if he hated both of us for his need. I did not give him the gift of tears or protestations and my only struggle was to cover my bruised flesh as soon as he was done.

He sneered at my haste. 'Suddenly so coy, mistress? You had best pray your husband will never return and discover you've played the harlot.'

I did not reply. My husband and kinsmen were safe beyond the reach of brigands who would put them to the sword or ship them in chains to be sold in Dublin. Only we were here at the strangers' mercy, or lack of it. And so it began: our winter of slavery.

They lived like kings at our expense. Only one thing we were able to keep secret: our tradition of gathering together for courage and solace. Though we could not join together as we wished we managed to meet in twos and threes in the fields, at the well or the kitchen and gained succour from mouthed incantations, pledges and signs. Our bodies they took by brute force. But our spirits, forged by the bloody deeds of the First Equinox from which we count our history, escaped domination.

Still, the presence of the Hunters in our midst was an ever troublesome thorn, pricking us into remembrance or our earlier lives and trials. My story was not unusual. I was brought here when I was a young child and mother's face unblemished. We had fled from the religious laws that our lords would not countenance. They would build their own church and live by laws drawn from the True Word. This place, we were told, was to be Heaven on earth. But the Elders' decrees were so many and severe that it was easy to fall foul of them. It was especially hard if a woman had the misfortune to be a natural beauty, like mother. For such as her were said to be marked out, divinely cursed, so that man could look on the embodiment of Eve's original sin. When father first suspected I too carried the stigma I was hurriedly given in marriage to Aelfric, harsh and thirty years my senior.

My marriage was less than a year old when a suspected thief was brought to ordeal. As was the custom he was made to grasp a red-hot iron and step out nine paces before his wounds were dressed. The bandages were to be unbound in a week: if the wounds were healing his innocence was proven, if septic he would be hanged. Mother visited him in secret and was dressing his hands with poultices when she was discovered. Father beat her for practising the Black Arts but still the Elders were not satisfied. She was denounced soon afterwards – accused of adultery with the man she'd helped. Although she swore her innocence before the altar it did not save her. As they dragged her away she swore revenge on all who wronged her kind.

She came back to us sadly changed. They gave her permission to live on the fringes of the settlement as an example to us. Poor mother: how she had dreaded her reflection.

While we would peek into the surface of the river on wash days, though such vanity was forbidden, she would busy herself gathering plants. Under her clever hands they would be dried and mashed into countless lotions and potions, according to our need. Her hair, which had grown grey overnight, was carefully plaited to hide the desecration beneath but there was no charm to draw the beholder's eye away from the splintered 'horn' of bone and gaping nostrils above her scarred lip. She drew more and more into silent meditation. Until one day she left here to live hermit-like in the caves over the mountain. Aelfric forbade me to ever see her but I was not the only one to brave my lord's wrath for love of her. She had helped and soothed at births and deaths and sick-beds. And she continued to counsel us.

'The men you fear are weak because they crave authority over each other. Plant an acorn of discord in their midst and it will flourish...'

So it was we began, timidly at first, to sow disharmony. A word here, a remark there about this man's holiness, that man's impiety, was all that was needed to set them at each other's throats. With their division came downfall and our freedom.

How could we have guessed we would lose it again short years later? The Hunters were different kinds of men. Tightly-bonded, they cared more for their brothers in arms than anything else. They seemed invincible, having lived by blade, bow and spear for so long. We dared not cross them or try and escape or we would be hunted down for their pleasure. How they loved setting out on their bloody pilgrimages and returning with carcasses slung over their horses' necks.

Each night, when Wulfstan finally let me be, I prayed to mother to come to me in spirit form and tell me what to do that we could be rid of them. My need for her gave my longing wings and she heard, as she always had. Even as Wulfstan moved uneasily in his sleep beside me the damp aura of the caves invaded my bedchamber and a scarred lip pressed tenderly against my ear.

She knew all and understood why we were sorely afraid that we would not survive another year. Because of our careful husbandry we had always had enough to eat in bounteous season and frozen. But now our pigs, goats and sheep were being slaughtered with no thought for the morrow. These men were not farmers, like my father and the followers of the old faith had been.

Our new tyrants had but one religion: hunting. Ill-served by the game birds and hares they killed in our woods they lusted for stags, fallow deer and wild boar. Now we began to tell of how our lost men-folk had journeyed to the heart of the deeply forested hillside yonder for their sport. Our sighs were heavy describing how the hooks in the kitchen beams had groaned with the weight of their burdens. It needed no great skill or subtlety to prey on their savage minds. When Wulfstan boasted to me of the bear, or wolf, he had slain in the past I praised him quickly, too easily, as one would a child trying to impress with fairy tales. Soon, they could think of nothing but embarking on a grand hunt. They lost the habit of watchfulness, making our task easier.

The night before they set out we sang as we took the last of the meat from our salt-barrels, showing we had faith in their ability to replenish our stocks. We marinated and cooked the flesh slowly before serving it out with great ceremony. I jostled with the others to ladle choice pieces out of the cauldron for Wulfstan. Since that first night he had wordlessly picked me out for his use alone. But this was the first time I had acknowledged his ownership.

In turn, he looked on me less coldly than usual. 'If there is good hunting tomorrow there will be good reason for us to stay all winter here, perhaps longer.'

'Do not doubt it,' I reassured him. 'There is much feasting to come.'

Two of the older girls, who had become favourites with the Hunters, were entrusted by us to lead the men to the edge of the forest. Of course, they did not lead them there directly but by tortuous routes: through dense thickets, up fern-choked hill-sides and down rock-strewn slopes splashed by gushing streams. The Hunters panted and toiled eagerly without complaint. They came to their task warm from our beds. At first light we had clung to their stirrups, pressing packages of dried food upon them, exhorting them to great things.

At last, they came, as we had promised, to the circle of standing stones at the mouth of the forest. They could almost taste victory as they paused to rest their horses and eat before entering the beckoning darkness. Faint howls and roars came from within and they greeted the sounds by pounding backs and boasting of the slaughter to be unleashed. They tore at their rations like wild animals, chewing, swallowing and gulping impatiently.

When the pain attacked it caught them unaware. They staggered around retching, so dizzy they barely knew ground from sky as they clutched at their vitals, or belts, trying to loosen and ease their agony. But the poison was swift and sure and one by one they fell paralysed to the ground.

We watched from the cave entrance safe in the knowledge that we could not be seen. Always in shadow and echoing with the incessant cries of ravens by day and swooping bats by night, the entrance is not easily visible, even when you have entered it a hundred times. Only when we were sure it was safe did we go down, dragging biers behind us. They stared at us in helpless amazement.

I squatted down by Wulfstan. 'Don't worry, my lord. You will be with us for the winter – and beyond.'

We have our husbands and fathers to thank for our livestock-keeping skills. The strongest among us can weave a pen from willow saplings as ably as any man. Not that the Hunters try to escape: how could they when they are hobbled to prevent them straying. Their horses are safe in the village getting used to yoke and plough. The natural rhythm of life has returned.

Mother remains in the cave. It is her choice to live in seclusion there, except for her charges. The once proud Hunters are fed, watered and tended by her just as my father and Aelfric used to be. I think some of them believe they will eventually be given freedom. Wulfstan does not deceive himself. Though he no longer has a tongue with which to curse me his eyes forever burn with terrible understanding and fury. I can see he remembers the flavoursome tit-bits I selected for his plate. He is not pleased about the impending birth though I have explained his proven ability to breed could prolong his life.

We have sacrificed two of their number so far at the place of stones. The first was in gratitude for our salvation and the other in humble petition that we who are large with child will bring forth girls. I am hopeful. Mother has prophesised that it will be so. And it is a propitious time for my pangs to quicken: with the harvest safely gathered in.

Michael Karwowski

Of French and Polish extraction, "French polish", Michael Karwowski is a self-employed public relations consultant, freelance journalist, and writer. Originally from Lancashire, where his father was a GP, he now lives and works in Bristol. He writes and reviews regularly for the subscription magazine, *Contemporary Review*, specialising in subjects including Bob Dylan, Tom Stoppard, and Harold Pinter, and was previously a regular contributor to *Plays and Players*. He is currently writing a book on the meaning of Bob Dylan's songs. 'The Goddaughter' is his first publication between book covers.

The Goddaughter

Michael Karwowski

Nicola asked her mother if I was a toilet. When she learned to read, she made out the word 'loo' on the toilet door, and my name is Louis: Nicola calls me Lou for short, and the difference between a 'u' and an 'o' is nothing to a child.

'No, Louis isn't a toilet,' her mother said, although I wouldn't be surprised if, under her breath, she'd added: 'but he can be a bit of a shit at times.'

Nicola is my goddaughter and my niece. 'Is that like 'nice'?' she asked me. Her mother spoke with the kind of accent that makes the two words sound alike.

'No,' I told her, 'it's not like 'nice'. 'Nice' rhymes with 'precise', 'niece' with 'geese'.

Nicola and I were friends, fellow conspirators, some said. During one of those interludes children have when they say No to everybody and everything, Nicola would not reply when I was mentioned. Teased with: 'Mummy?' she would reply: 'No,' with a pronounced shake of the head. 'Daddy?' 'No.' 'Granddad?' 'No.' 'Granny?' 'No.' 'Uncle Lou?' Silence, stillness.

Nicola and I saw a lot of each other. I had more or less retired at 30 and was living at my parents' house, and, with her parents both working, Nicola would spend the day with us.

I lived in the attic, a tiny room with a skylight. Because there was no heating up there, I called it 'Siberia'.

'Where are you going?' Nicola would ask me whenever I went upstairs. 'To

Siberia,' I would reply. 'Can I come too?' she would say; and sometimes, when I wasn't writing, I would say: 'Yes.'

I was writing a book in my retirement, a philosophical work on the nature of reality. Coincidentally, layabouts and parasites sometimes use this as an excuse for doing nothing, which probably accounts for the fact that I was generally regarded as a layabout and parasite.

'Are you a roundabout?' Nicola asked me. 'Mummy told Daddy that you were a bit of a roundabout.'

'Did she?' I said.

'Yes, and a paragraph.'

'Site!' Nicola looked blankly at me.

'Parasite!'

'Yes. Are you?'

We were outside at the time. I got her to sit down, picked her up by the heels and twirled her round and round. She held her arms above her head, letting herself go. But then some marbles she had in a pocket fell out and she began to cry. I put her down, took her up into my arms. She clung to me.

'Now you're a parasite,' I said, 'and before you were a roundabout.'

She looked serious. 'What's a parasite?'

'You clinging to me,' I said, 'me to you, somebody holding onto somebody else.'

She laughed at the idea of me in her own cuddled state.

'You're not a baby,' she said. 'I can be,' I said.

When invited, Nicola would follow me up the steep, narrow stairs to my attic. While I looked through the skylight at the clouds or made notes on my observations, she would play with a little toy dog, built around a skeleton of strings, that could be made to do almost anything simply by pushing up a piece of cork to which the strings were attached.

Tiring of this, she'd say: 'I love you,' to attract my attention.

I'd reply: 'Naturally,' or not at all.

Then Nicola would become thoughtful, screwing up her face with the effort of concentration, before beginning a sentence, stopping, beginning another, stopping, then, hesitantly, ask me one of her eternal questions.

'Is it true that God is a piece of shit?' she asked me once.

I looked at her.

'Arthur said that God was a piece of shit,' she explained.

'Who's Arthur?' I asked.

'The boy next door,' she said.

'God isn't, no,' I said. 'But some people say that 'man' is.'

She looked puzzled.

'What comes out when you go to the toilet?' I asked, by way of explanation.

'Wee,' she said.

'Yes, and what else?'

She brightened. 'Shit!'

'Yes, we're full of shit, see. That's why some people say that 'man' is a piece of shit.'

Needless to say, Nicola's parents didn't take too kindly to my godfatherliness, particularly after one occasion when, looking like an angel in her white frock and pink ribbons, surrounded by simpering guests at a dinner party, Nicola had suddenly announced: 'Lou says we're full of shit.'

This *faux pas* led to the unanimous decision that I was a bad influence on the girl. Nicola and I would have to be kept apart. A babysitter was found.

'Why can't I go to Granny's like before?' Nicola wanted to know. Her parents had decided that honesty was the best policy.

'We don't think it's good for you to see your Uncle Louis,' her father told her. 'He's not always a nice man; and we want you to be a good girl.'

'Why isn't he nice?' Nicola asked.

'You see, Nicola, there's a right way and a wrong way to act,' he explained. 'And we want you to act in the right way. And the way your Uncle Louis encourages you to behave isn't the right way.'

'Is it the wrong way?' she asked.

Her father was reluctant to condemn his brother out of hand.

'No...o...o...o,' he said, hesitantly, 'not exactly, but it's not the right way.'

The babysitter's notions of cleanliness were not their own, however. After an initial period of spic and span, they'd come home to a daughter with dirty hands, dirty face, and dishevelled clothes. Nicola was left with us again while they looked for somebody more suitable. My father, Nicola's grandfather, was dying of an incurable disease. He'd lie all day in the large double bed in the master bedroom, too exhausted to do much more than sleep or stare at the ceiling. Nicola would be left with him while my mother went about her household chores.

'Doesn't he ever *do* anything?' she asked me. 'No,' I replied. 'Why not?' 'Because he's dying.'

She considered this for a moment, then: 'The room where he is, where he's lying, is it the dying room?'

I looked at her.

'Like the living room, but for dying in?'

'Yes, I suppose it is,' I said.

My father was too weak to go to the toilet, so he'd relieve himself into a commode. My mother would usher Nicola out of the room while this was going on, but sometimes she left my father to it and the door was unguarded so that there was nothing to stop Nicola going in, my father being largely indifferent to his surroundings.

Once, when she came in as he was relieving his bowels, I was in the room. Glancing towards him, she gave me a significant look. Later, she climbed the stairs to my room, knocked on the door, and, invited in, entered.

'Lou?' she began.

'Yes?'

'Lou, what's dying?'

'Dying?' I hesitated. 'Dying's the opposite of living. It means you disappear as a person, you go away for good.'

'Where do you go?'

'Nowhere; you stop going somewhere; you just drain away into nothing, like water down the drain.'

'But if you go nowhere, don't you stay where you are?' I considered this, then: 'Yes, I suppose you do.'

'Don't you *know*, then?' Nicola asked abruptly.

'Know? No,' I said. 'I don't know. Grown-ups might pretend that they know it all. I suppose they want to impress the kids so that they'll do what they want them to. But they don't know much, really. They know how to pretend they know, that's about all. Children sometimes know more than grown-ups.'

She looked her in amazement.

'But I'm a children,' she said.

'You're a child,' I said. 'But, yes, I mean you might know more, too.

There was a silence, then: 'You know you said we're full of shit?' she said.

'Yes.'

'And that someone said we *are a* piece of shit?'

'Yes.'

'Do we shit ourselves away, then? Do we shit and shit and shit and shit until there's nothing left?'

She'd already commented on the fact that her grandfather had been getting noticeably thinner for some time.

I laughed. 'What an idea!' I said. 'Yes, perhaps we do.'

Soon after this, my father died. A portent, although we didn't recognise it as such at the time, came in his urgent need to relieve his bowels. With the approach of death, all his muscles were relaxing, including those of his bowels. Since he'd eaten hardly anything for days, we tried to persuade him that he was mistaken. But, in his enfeebled way, he managed to so insist that my mother and I placed him onto the commode: he almost filled it. Two hours later, he was dead.

Spirited away by the undertaker, he was brought back in a coffin, which was placed in the living room.

Nicola asked if she might see him. My mother, taking this as an expression of the child's attachment to her grandfather, consented. I accompanied her to the coffin-side, lifted the face-cloth. Gravely, she looked in. She was immediately struck by his deathly pallor.

'Why is he so white?' she asked.

I was about to explain, when she offered her own explanation: 'Is it that he's all sh...?'

'Sh!' I said quickly.

'Why?' she asked. 'I don't know,' I confessed.

The family had always lived in the same house, but I'd only recently come to know the lie of the land. As a boy, I'd been familiar with the area in much the same way that a human being is familiar with his own person. On my return, though, I'd begun to explore it, and, gradually, to know it in a different way: in the way a pathologist knows the human body. Starting with long walks in the surrounding hills, I'd slowly worked my way inwards, moving in ever-decreasing circles.

Nicola was keen to accompany me on these jaunts. To begin with, she'd be tired after a few hundred yards, miles and miles to her little legs, and eager to go back. But, with experience, she was able to go further, until she could actually climb to the very top of the hill behind the house, from where she could survey the hills before her, or turn to look at the plain left behind.

On some of these walks, I'd take the family pet, an Alsatian bitch named Roger, experiencing an absurd delight in exercising the fat off her.

Whenever I'm pleased with myself, I can't help testifying to my complacency by repeated expressions of satisfaction. Thus, I'd say to Nicola: 'The good thing is that Roger is getting such a good run,' or: 'I can't tell you how pleased I am that Roger is getting so much exercise,' or: 'I'm glad about Roger, anyway.'

I'd use one or all of these formulae, or any number of variations, until I was sick almost to death with the tedium of it all. But I couldn't help myself.

At first, Nicola said nothing. Then, one afternoon, after a long silence, she suddenly asked: 'When's Roger going to die?'

Caught by surprise, I pondered an answer. Finally, I said: 'She should live for a few years yet,' adding as an afterthought: 'unless she dies before her time.'

Nicola considered this, then: 'How could she die before her time?' she asked.

'If someone kills her,' I said, explaining: 'There's death from natural causes; that's when you die because you're too old to live, or because you're sick; and then there's death by design; that's when you kill yourself or someone kills you.'

It was about this time that Nicola began calling me 'Dad'. I pointed out to her that I wasn't her father, but her uncle. In her turn, though, she pointed out that I was her godfather, and wasn't that a father of a kind?

'I don't know if I qualify as your godfather,' I replied. 'A godfather's supposed to give his godchild something for her christening. I never gave you anything.'

She waited patiently until I'd finished, then, slowly and distinctly, as if speaking to a child, she said: 'Yes, but you take me for walks and you tell me things.'

'Don't your parents tell you things?' I asked.

'They tell me not to do things that you shouldn't do... and to do things that you should,' she replied, pondering her words for a moment, before adding: 'Dad... why should you do those things?'

'What things?'Save up your pennies, brush your hair, say your prayers, things like that?' I remained silent.

Shortly after this, Nicola's parents finally found a babysitter they considered suitable and Nicola ceased to spend so much time with us. But she continued to figure prominently in my life; for if I saw little of her, I seemed to hear of nothing else.

'Mary says you've ruined that girl's life,' my mother announced one tea-time. 'She says you've filled her up with so much nonsense that she doesn't know where she is.'

Mary was my sister-in-law, Nicola's mother.

'She used to be such a happy child,' my mother went on, 'and now Mary says she's full of misery. What did you do to her?'

'Nothing,' I replied. 'She asked me questions and sometimes I answered them.'

'Yes, but how? That's the point. You have to be careful with a child. You can't tell her everything. You could ruin her chances of happiness forever.'

The next I heard about it was from Nicola's father, Joe. 'Nicola's as thin as one of those famine victims,' he began, pointedly. 'She eats hardly anything at all. She seems so depressed; and she used to be such a happy child.'

I didn't reply.

He waited for a few moments before adding: 'All this thinking's very well, but does it make you happy? I mean, that's the point, isn't it?'

Mary was less sympathetic.

'People like you should be put away,' she said.

'Where?' I asked.

'Somewhere safe like Siberia,' she answered.

They were soon offered further cause for criticism. My mother, depressed by my father's death, took an overdose of sleeping tablets. Preoccupied with my book, I noticed nothing unusual. But Mary, calling in during her lunch break, saw that the bedroom curtains were still drawn and, running upstairs to find out why, discovered her mother-in-law in a coma. Rushed to hospital, her stomach was emptied out.

'I hope you're satisfied now,' were Mary's first words to me after the event.

'First Nicola, then your own mother. I wouldn't be surprised if you'd had something to do with your father's death. You're an angel of death, do you know that?'

Such scathing comments soon became the order of the day.

'It's subversives like you,' Mary went on at our next meeting, "professional thinkers",' – this in a tone of withering sarcasm and followed by a humourless laugh – 'who're the ultimate cause of all the troubles in society; or you would be,'– pause for effect – 'if you could actually finish anything! You undermine values, dispense with morals. It's as simple as that. You want to destroy everything, but what will you put in its place? That's the question. What? Tell me. Go on!'

I didn't reply.

'You don't answer because you've got nothing to put in its place; that's it, isn't it? Destroy everything and put nothing in its place: blueprint for paradise, I *don't* think!'

I couldn't help joining in with her laughter.

'Yes, it's easy to laugh when you don't have to earn a living; you've got all the time in the world to laugh. Clown!'

Soon after this, I saw Nicola again when she popped in with her parents to see my mother. I was in the attic when she arrived. Nicola was warned not to leave the living-room, but when her mother's attention was distracted, she took the opportunity to come up to see me. She entered without knocking. We looked at each other.

'Dad...?' she began.

'Yes?'

'Dad, why... why is something unnatural? I mean, what's natural?'

I considered this, then: 'It depends on the context,' I said. 'I mean, why do you ask? What's behind the question?'

'There was something on television,' she explained, 'on the News; and Mummy told Daddy that it was unnatural.'

'I see,' I said. 'Well, nothing's unnatural, really. Everything that's done is natural, because if something wasn't natural it wouldn't be done.'

'Why did she say that it was unnatural, then?'

'She meant that it wasn't natural so far as *she* was concerned, it was unnatural for *her*, it wasn't in *her* nature to do whatever it was.'

'But if I...?'

'Yes, if something's natural for you, then it *is* natural.'

'So everything...?'

'Yes, everything's natural.'

She seemed relieved. 'Right!' she said.

She went back downstairs. I stayed in my attic.

In the small hours of the following morning, I was woken by a ring on the doorbell. I waited to see if my mother would go. Again the doorbell rang. I heard some movement below, then my mother's loud whisper: 'Louis, there's someone at the door.'

Sighing, I got out of bed and went down. My mother was waiting at the bottom of the stairs. As I reached her, there was another ring on the doorbell. I went to open the door. Nicola was standing on the step, alone.

'Who is it?' my mother asked from behind me.

'Nicola,' I said.

'Hello, Dad,' she said.

'Come in,' I replied.

'What is it?' my mother asked apprehensively. 'Nicola, where are your Mummy and Daddy? You're not alone, are you?'

Nicola glanced at her before turning to me.

'They're dead,' she said.

There was a gasp from my mother.

'Are you sure?' I asked. 'How are they dead? How did they die?'

'From natural causes,' she said.

'Natural causes!' my mother repeated in a tone of horrified disbelief.

'Yes,' said Nicola.

My mother let out another gasp. We turned to look at her.

Fran Landsman

Fran Landsman is an award-winning documentary film-maker, currently taking a year out to do an MA in creative writing at Bath Spa University. She is writing her first book, a collection of linked short stories called *Britannia Terrace*. Her films include *My Family And Autism*, *The Waughs - Fathers And Sons*, *The Secret Life Of The Classroom*, *The Piano – A Love Affair*, and *Barnardo's Children*. She trained as a journalist, and worked on newspapers and magazines before becoming a television researcher on the Parkinson Show. Now she has two children and lives with her husband in Bath.

Life Sucks

Fran Landsman

I was just seventeen when I experienced the worst day of my life so far. I was working as a junior at Shirley's Salon and the morning started with mangy hair clippings up my nose, and talk of colostomy bags. It went downhill from there.

By two o'clock I'd walked out, convinced that being a hairdresser was second only to working in an abattoir, but more boring … and without the protective doming, I decided they could stick their apprenticeship in hair dressing NVQ level two down the plughole.

I was musing on my future, or lack of it, as I walked home along Britannia Terrace in the trendy end of Bath. Now I was no longer likely to become a stylist to the stars I recalled the other options the school careers advisor had placed before me. Nursing? No, too much death. The army? No, too much death. The bank? I'd rather die. Road Protester seemed the favourite option as I turned the key in our front door.

I thought Mum and Dad would still be at work, so I jumped out of my skin when I walked into the lounge to see this strange woman lounging on our sofa. She shot up and stood with her back to me. All I noticed was the grotesque orange line of make-up that stopped at her jaw bone, her hair was up in a pony tail, and her clothes were like something you might see on a haberdashery assistant in Debenhams.

'Oh, excuse me,' I said, as if this wasn't my own house, then I realised that I'd walked in on a scene that was so freaky, so deviant and disgusting that all I could do was stand there.

My father looked shocked to see me home early, but his horror *was nothing* compared with mine. That was how it seemed anyway, but then I wasn't concerned with his feelings at that moment. We just stared at each other, for what seemed like an age.

'What the hell is going on here?' I said eventually.

'Janine. Christ, Janine. Oh God – I'm sorry.'

He fell back onto the sofa and sat with his legs apart so that the tight black skirt crept up his lap and I could see that bit of his tights where they go a deeper colour at the top. The prim white nylon blouse was buttoned up to the neck so there *was no cleavage* on view, but he had tits. I could see the bra through the thin material. My dad had tits. Jesus. They were bigger than mine.

I stood there gawping as he flew out of the room, or should I say hobbled on his red stiletto shoes. His outfit was ridiculous. He'd even co-ordinated his red shoes with a stretchy red belt that I knew to be mine. He crashed into the downstairs loo and locked the door.

'That's my fucking belt,' I yelled. 'MY FUCKING BELT.'

I ran up to my room and threw myself on the bed, scattering the various stuffed animals I'd been meaning to chuck for ages. I cried for a while and jammed the same few swear words over and over again into my pillow. 'You bastard. You fucking bastard. Fuck you – you bastard.' Eventually I turned onto my back exhausted and stared at the ceiling.

I'd come home expecting a bit of compassion because my career had hit the lino before it had even got started. It was my Dad who would have been sympathetic. He'd have said I was too good to work there anyway, and it was their loss. That's what he was like. At least it was, until he turned into one of Cinderella's shit-face siblings. I didn't know what to do. My Dad was the one person who had always made things okay again when life sucked. I had always adored my Dad. He was kind and gentle and funny, and always there when I needed someone to talk to. Now where was he? I asked myself. In the downstairs bog slipping off his tights for all I knew.

I sat up and rifled in my handbag for my secret stash of cigarettes. I wasn't allowed to smoke, but it occurred to me that he'd have a job telling me what to do now. It was only then that I thought about my mother. She'd be bound to divorce him after this. I'd be a broken homer like most of my friends. I used to think they were lucky because they got double pocket money, but they all thought I was the lucky one. Was that irony or paradox? I knew I should have paid more attention in English.

I lit up and took a deep drag. As I blew the smoke directly into the glass eyes of a flea-bitten teddy I had a realisation. It just thwacked me in the chest and set me off crying so hard that I could hardly catch my breath.

Aunty Christine. Aunty bleeding Christine. Aunty sodding fucking Christine.

I don't remember when it started happening. It was all I'd ever known. Every evening my Dad came home from his job as a computer programmer, went upstairs, and then down came Aunty Christine. I loved to play with her while Mum cooked. She was tall and eccentric and her cheeks and lips were the rosiest colour I'd ever seen. Mum always looked pale in comparison to Aunty Christine. She had dinner with us every evening and we chatted and watched TV, just like a normal family. I never asked where Dad had gone. I just thought that it was what Dads did.

One day when I was about five, I remember because I'd just started school, I went for tea to a friend's house. It was then I discovered that this was not what all Dads did. When I got home I asked Mum where Dad went at night. I've forgotten what she said, but I do know that the next night Dad had dinner with us and I never saw Aunty Christine again. Of course I asked where she was. They said something or other, but even at that age I just knew not to ask again. The subject was closed.

Did I suspect something? I don't know. I can't believe now that I didn't recognise him, but I was so young, and I had no reason to suspect something weird was happening. Aunty Christine had long blonde hair. My Dad was dark. She left lipstick marks on the glasses, which I thought very lady-like, and her skin was powdery. Lord knows what he did with his stubble. I think she did have a deep voice, now I think about it. But how was I to know?

Occasionally, as I grew up, ideas would come to me to explain Dad's past disappearances. I crossed off burglar straight away as we never had much money. Werewolf was a favourite for a while and I even went so far as to look for fang marks on my mother's neck. Eventually I just forgot about it.

The next twelve years were pretty ordinary really. I went to school and picked my spots and flounced around like you do. If there was anything unusual, it was just how much I adored my Dad. We did stuff together. Not big stuff, just watching telly or cooking, but we talked. My Mum was not as much fun, but I know she loved me. I didn't have anything to complain about really. In fact I always wanted to run away because it sounded exciting, but I just didn't have a reason. Anyway, they'd really sorted that omission. Now I had issues my friends hadn't even dreamt of.

As I lay on my bed that afternoon I was still at the stage of feeling sorry for myself and furious with him. Then I heard a tap on the door.

'Go away.'

'Janine? Janine love? Can I come in? Please let me come in and explain.'

'If you can explain high heels and a skirt – and MY belt – I'd like to hear it.'

He came into my room and knelt by my bed. 1 remember feeling relieved that he'd put his own clothes back on, and when I told him this he looked me *in the eyes.*

'Those are my clothes.'

'Not that fucking belt. That's not yours,' I said, giving the belt an importance that I fully realised it didn't deserve. I just didn't know what else to say.

'No,' he said. 'I thought it was your mother's. It was in our room.'

I remembered her borrowing it then, but I still couldn't let it go.

'You had no right.'

'No,' he said.

'I'm a transvestite, Janine. I'm sorry, I don't want to be this way and I wish I wasn't, but I am. I'd rather that you just never found out, but it's too late for that now. I love you, Janine. I'm so sorry. Please don't hate me. I'm still the same person – still your Dad.'

'You are not the same person. You are NOT. I want my Dad.'

Just saying that made me cry all over again.

'How could you?' I said over and over. 'How could you? How could you?'

'It's not something I chose.'

'If you loved me you wouldn't do that. It's weird. It's… I don't know… it's perverted.'

I was shivering and he tried to touch my arm. It felt like I'd been stung. I wanted to stick the knife in and twist. Why me? Why my Dad? Even when I saw his eyes fill up I didn't leave off. I couldn't stop now.

'Go on, cry. That's what girls do – and you want to be a girl.' We were quiet for a while. My head was spinning and I felt sick. Then suddenly another thing occurred to me.

'And what did you think you were doing getting married and having a child eh? Obviously Mum knows seeing as we spent five years having dinner with *Aunty Christine.* How could she? You're disgusting. You're both disgusting.'

I was gabbling now. I wanted to calm down but words were just vomiting out of my mouth. I couldn't stop them. I couldn't bear to see his face looking at me for another minute.

'Get out my room. GET OUT.'

He got off his knees and walked towards my door with a poster of Pete Burns on it. Then he turned towards me and said he wasn't going to lose me.

'You already have,' I told him. At that moment I knew I had the power to grind him into the dirt. It was either that or collapse into a puddle of tears and snot. 'Shut the door behind you … *Aunty Christine*', I said with the hardest voice I could muster. He shut the door and I hurled every stupid teddy I could find after him.

I didn't come out of my room again that night. I heard my mother come home from work in the evening and I heard them arguing, but much as I tried, I couldn't make out what they were saying. When Mum knocked on my door I just yelled at her to go away and, unlike Dad, she did. I lay on my bed and watched the car headlights make shadows travel round my room, just as they had when I was little… when I was happy.

The next day I could tell by the noises around the house that Dad hadn't gone to work, and there was no way I was setting foot in Shirley's again, so I kept to my room. I felt really tired, and much calmer. Sort of all cried out. It suddenly occurred to me to Google 'transvestite' and there was tons of stuff about it. You've never met one in your life, and suddenly the world is full of them. Anyway, I had to admit it didn't seem as revolting as I'd thought. It appeared they just got a kick out of wearing women's gear. Cross-dressing they called it. They didn't really grow tits and lots of them were married with children. I found that hard to believe, but it got me thinking.

I looked towards the clothes that lay around my floor – jeans, boots, even a leather waistcoat I'd nicked off Dad. It occurred to me that I'd voted for a tranny to win on Big Brother, and Lily Savage was a man. They looked good though. My Dad looked like a right wanker. He's six foot, muscular and handsome and he looked way better in jeans than a pencil skirt. He had longish hair too which I'd always thought was cool till I saw it up in a scrunchy. He rode a motorbike for fuck's sake.

There was one boy at school who was a bit of a weirdo, but I liked him and I thought he might understand. He never used to speak to anyone but he was well fit, and that summer we' d started meeting up on the allotments at the back of our terrace. He was the sort of person who I absolutely trusted to keep a secret, and I needed support here. I decided to phone him from under the bed covers.

'Tom? Is that you?'

'Why are you whispering?'

'Because you have to swear on your mother's life that if I tell you something you'll never, ever tell a soul.'

'OK. What is it?'

'My father is a tranny.'

'A radio?'

'A transvestite – A trans-fucking-vestite.'

'Is that it?'

'What do you mean, is that it? That's bloody fucking big.'

'My father is autistic. That's bloody fucking big.'

'Jesus, is no one normal? Shall we run away?'

'Can't.'

'Life sucks doesn't it?'

We talked till I realised that I actually could find it within me to see the funny side of the situation. This wasn't boring. This made me special. It had only been twenty-four hours and already I was getting over the biggest trauma of my life. I was feeling pretty damn mature by the time I went downstairs to find my Dad.

Maturity dissolved when I walked into the kitchen and found both parents sat at the kitchen table looking haggard. It flashed through my head that I had a choice whether to be rude, high and mighty, angry, casual… in fact I just burst into tears and they both hugged me for a while.

'Ask me whatever you want,' Dad said.

'Why do you do it?'

'I need to. It makes me happy,' he told me.

I turned to Mum. 'How can you bear it?'

'I used to think it was weird, but I just got used to it. If you love someone you just have to let them be who they are, and it's not as if I didn't know when we got married. I just decided to cope with it. It's an obsession,' she said, 'and as obsessions go, it's not as bad as football.' She laughed at her joke, but I failed to see the connection.

I turned to my Dad again. 'You're a biker. You're a bloke.'

'I know, Janine. But even bikers like to get dressed up. They get a kick out of pretending to be someone tough and dangerous for a while, then they go back to being who they are. It's not that different.'

'It's a bit different to me. But OK, you've just got to tell me you'll stop.'

'I can't.'

'For me?'

'No.'

That all happened a few months ago now, and I've never actually seen him dress up since then. But things have changed. At the moment I still think he's a selfish bastard, but that seems Mum's problem now – and I'm in love with Tom. I'm really in love with Tom.

He assured me he'd never be seen dead in a skirt, but he had been known to talk to invisible people. 'Hey,' I said, 'I can handle that.'

Nick Law
When Nick was about seven years old he wrote a story called Dr Who and the Octomen (men in robotic suits that had eight extendable arms - little knowing that a certain Mr Stan Lee had already conceived half of it) and was made to go class to class reading it out for the benefit of the rest of the school. He loved it – a legend in his own milk-break. He wanted to be a writer. Thirty-five years later and he is again as pleased as punch to be picked for this anthology.

Virtue In Danger

or a London Spark is put out.

A Moral Tale of Bordellos, Boxing and Bristol Pluck

Nick Law

Bartholomew Rakehell went out on a jaunt
To the Brothels of Bankside – his usual haunt.
In Bawdy-House Alley he came to a stoppe
At Mrs Come-Quickly's – his favourite shoppe
Where the Swells and the Fancy would oft' spend the nights
After drinkin' and gamblin' at Boodles or Whites.
Her Wenches were comely, her rooms clean and tidy
Her Virgins were all guaranteed Bona Fide.
She'd ripe juicy slatterns like Lombardy Grapes
Some Buxom, some lithesome – all sizes and shapes.
Some Doxies were skilled in Particular Ways:
Miss Payne had a talent for Le Vice Anglais!
With Whip, Cane and Paddle she battered men's bums
Her beatings made Debauchees cry for their Mums.
Miss Suckling, who, versed in the Art of Fellatio
Could gobble a p—k regardless of Ratio,
Bore off her patrons on Spumey Adventures

Due, on the whole, to complete lack of dentures.
Equally good, tho' not with her Gums
Miss Palm was a Marvel with fingers and thumbs.
Through dexterous digits she turned Floppadicks
From limp lettuce-leaves into Celery Sticks!
There was also the Trollop they all called Black Peg
On account of her hair – and the odd wooden leg.
Which was shap'd like a Dildoe and thro' quiet Winters
Was as good as a Man – apart from the splinters.

But Rakehell's insatiable Hunger was for
A fresh Country maid, not some clapp'd out old Wh—e
So 'twas Rosie he pick'd and then pluck'd and deflower'd
But her Scented Embraces he sullied and sour'd.
A cruel, Vicious man, he used her with force
And show'd not a jot of regret or remorse.
'No time like the First time' he bellow'd with Pride
As Rosie just lay there all wither'd and cried.
'Here's twenty-five guineas' he said to the mother
'And twenty-five more if you furnish another.
Let her be fair and fifteen years of age
Bring her tomorrow: I'll Double the wage!'

Next morn' went the Bawd to find him a mate
She took along ribbands and lace as her bait
To the Gardens of Vauxhall to seek out her Prey:
Innocent lasses just out for the day.
There by the Fountains she spotted a girl
With hair like Spun Gold and skin white as pearl.
Standing alone all agog at the Sights
In London for probably one or two nights,
Not yet corrupted by City Diversions
She was just perfect for Rakehell's Perversions.

'Good day, dear sweet child' the old Mistress said
'Are you newly arriv'd? Have you board? Have you bed?
If not, there's a place that I recommend

The rent's somewhat dear but you'll not need to spend
The least 'Bit o' Blunt' – I mean money – you see
I own the Establishment. Come, allow me
To give you these Prettying Trifles to wear.
Here's lace for your stomacher, silk for your hair
And if you come later I'll give you a cap.
Shall we say Eight o' clock? Very good. Here's a Map!'

Well, Jenny was taken aback safe to say
But she bobbed a neat curtsy and answer'd 'Good day.
'Tis true I am new 'ere. From Bristol I've come.
Your kindness is such that I'm almost struck dumb.
I don't know no-one and have nowhere to stay.
How Lucky I am to have met you today.
Your generous offer I'd gladly accept
But how'd I repay you? I'd be in your debt.'
'I'll think of a way,' said the Beldam 'don't fear.
Just come as arranged. Now there's a good dear.'

The stroke of Eight chimed with a knock at the door
'She'll enter a Maid but she'll leave as a Wh—e'
Cackled Mrs Come-Quickly the raddled old B—ch
Thinking of how, in an hour, she'd be rich.
In came Poor Jen and was shown to a room
Little suspecting she went to her Doom.
The Villain was waiting, The Trap had been set,
Just like a linnet caught in a net
Was how she'd been snared that day i' th' park
And now, far from home, she stood i' th' dark.
Lighting a candle to find out the bed
What did she see, but the Mad Grinning head
Of Bartholomew Rakehell. 'Sweetheart' he cried
'Tonight is our Wedding-Night. You are my Bride!
So Off with your Stays and Out with your Bubbies
And On with the game of Wifeys and Hubbies!'
He Grabb'd her and held her tight. Harder and tighter
But lo and behold, Little Jen was a Fighter!

Bred down in Bristol, her father'd won Prizes.
The Art of the Pugilist held no surprises.
She twist'd and turn'd him and landed a Jab
He shriek'd like a Molly, he cried like a Bab.
With Scientifik Precision she rain'd down her blows
The rake tried to counter – she Bloodyed his Nose!
Thirty-Two rounds worth of combat in One
Such were the flurry of Hits that she won.
Feignin' and feintin' with Flicks of her wrists
She taught him a lesson with Knuckles and Fists.
Finally Beaten, Batter'd and Bruis'd
His wits were all Muddled his senses confus'd
So forgettin' the rules and defyin' the odds
She gave him a Plum one – right in the Cods!

Mrs Come-Quickly on hearin' his cries
Couldn't believe it and shriek'd 'D—n my eyes
If the Slut ain't the best that I've ever heard.
He's never made That noise before, 'pon my word!'
And started to think of the Money she'd make
From selling the girl to Rake after Rake.

Meanwhile, in the chamber, Jen scoop'd up his Gold
While Bartholomew lay on the floorboards out cold.
Then out o' th' window climb'd brave Little Jen
The Victorious Slayer of Miscreant Men.
Next day, Rakehell scream'd when he look'd i' th' glass
For his eyes were as Black as Beelzebub's A—e!
His Deforméd nose was like that o' Cyrano
The low blow had turn'd him from Bass to Soprano.
So off went the Blackguard a-limpin' with Pain
Neither he nor his B——ks were e'er seen again.

As for Jenny Go-Sprightly who'd snatched up the gold
Of Bartholomew Rakehell, that Villain so bold,
And escaped from the evil old Harriden's Den
Of Iniquity, Coitus and Deviant Men,

The City of Bristol was where she was bound
For that was the place where her Home could be found.
Her father, a Taverner, ran the King's Head
Tho' chiefly for Prizefighting he had been bred.
He'd fought No Neck, The Butcher, The Battling Jew,
Nacker Jack and Jack Cabbage, to name but a few
And tho' never a Champion, it has to be said,
A True Bristol man from his toes to his head.
Now Jenny, that Chip from her father's old Block
Had escaped from the brothel at Nine o'th'clock.
Only to find that the last Coach had left
Leaving her Stranded, Forlorn and Bereft.
Alone once again was the poor pretty maid
When the kindly old Innkeeper came to her aid.
'Come in from the cold' said the wizen'd Old Prune
'You may stay here the night e'en tho' there's no room
For I'll give you my bed and sleep on the floor
'Tho' I may keep you up all night long – as I snore.
Have some supper and sit by the fire, my dear.'
Said the liquorish Old Goat with a wink and a leer.
'Your troubles are over – no need to be glum.'
'Your kindness is such that I'm almost struck dumb
I'll have to repay you. I'll be in your debt'
Said Jen, with a sigh, knowing what she would get.
But seeing that there could be no other way
She agreed. After all, it had been a long day.
Jenny woke the next morning rested, refresh'd
She stretch'd and she yawn'd then got up and got dress'd.
She stepp'd o'er the Innkeeper led on the floor
Who'd been there all night - just the way that he'd swore.
As quiet as a church mouse as pure as The Pope
Helped, there's no doubt, by the gag and the rope.
Then off on her Journey went Jen with a laugh
And the coach bounc'd along toward Bristol and Bath.

Her Travelling Companions along for the ride
Were: a fat florid Alewife, 'bout two Hogsheads wide

87

Her pale reedy Sister, who most of the time
Bore a countenance like she was sucking a lime.
(Stand them together thought mischievous Jen
And they'd look without doubt like a large number 10.)
A vain preening Dandy, all powder and frills
A dewlapp'd old Quack, all nostrums and pills
And also a Parson, who (easy to tell)
'Tho preaching of Heaven, was destin'd for Hell.
The countryside sounds of cuckoos and crickets
Passed pleasantly by until Maidenhead Thickets!
A Notorious place where Footpads would ply
Their Nefarious trade with a Shot and a Cry
Of 'Stand and Deliver' the Highwayman's Call
Tho' the chances of robb'ry in daylight were small.
'Stand and Deliver!' a sudden voice said
'Or ye'll all feel me Pistols and choke on me lead!
I'll Strip ye all naked and give ye both Barrells
I'll dance on your Graves while I sing Christmas Carols!'
Well, the men sh–t their breeches, the women all spew'd
(While Jen kiss'd goodbye all the cash she'd accrued.)
The carriage was ringing with Screaming and sobs
Wet, tear-stained cheeks and trembling Gobs
Whimpers of 'O Lord please save us, Amen'
Fainting Hysterics – and that was the men!
The Alewife was nervously guzzling gin
The Sister was stuck in her chair like a pin
The Doctor was sick, the Parson blasphemed
The Dandy's whole wardrobe would have to be cleaned.

Up to the window the Highwayman leapt
Those in the carriage cowered and wept.
Murthering eyes like those of a Viper
Peer'd from under his hat and over his Wiper.
Brandishing pistols he leant in the coach
Snarling 'I'll take that pocket-watch. Hand o'er that brooch!
I'll wager Ten guineas to one single groat
Ye've never before met a better Cut-Throat.

And just to be sure it's the end of your trip
I'd be much obleeged if ye'd get out and Strip!'
And so they alighted, each one of the pack
The Alewife, her Sister, the Fop and the Quack
The Parson, the Coachman, and Jen at the rear
The Highwayman stopped her and lull'd in her ear:
'Sweet Flower rest sure that I mean you no harm
Mais sans Pétales vous n'appellerez pas l'Alarme.'

'All thieves rot in Hell and you'll hang with your brothers!'
Spat the Alewife, attempting to cover her Udders.
Which wasn't so easy whilst swatting at bees
That, and the fact that they hung to her Knees.
By contrast her Sister, the family Runt
Was all skin and bones with a back like her front.
Standing alongside the Miss and the Madam
The Parson was clutching an oak-leaf, like Adam.
The Doctor, 'twas plain, had a Dose of the clap
And the Dandy just sat there all covered in crap.
The Coachman was equally naked of course
And bless'd with a Tackle that rivalled his Horse.

Now Jen to behold was a Marvellous sight
Her hair was all Golden, her skin milky-white
And as soft as a flurry of Feathers or Flakes.
Her sun-dappled breasts were like Sally Lunn's cakes.
She made such a Show that you could have sold Tickets
For e'en just a glimpse of *her* Maidenhead Thickets.
The Highwayman gazed at this Beauty of Bristol
A Lassie to put lead in any man's Pistol
And gave her a wink once he'd sated his greed
Then leapt from the ground and mount'd his steed.

'I'll wager a Groat to anyone's Guinea
I'll Kill the first cove that escapes from this spinney'
The Bold Villain cried as he dug in his spurs
Leaving them there like a pack o' Wild Curs.

To tell of the way that Jen finally reach'd Home
Cannot be Encompass'd in one single Poem.
But suffice it to say the Adventures she had
Were Bitter and Sweet and Happy and Sad
And while passing through Wiltshire dress'd as a boy
She was greatly mistook for a Hobble-de-Hoy.
Which came as a Shock to one fusty old Lord
To discover a Scabbard instead of a Sword!'
But one way or another she reach'd the King's Head
And her overjoy'd father (who thought she was dead!)
Back to the land of Stingo and Smoke
Home once again amongst Genial Folk.

'Twas only days later while pouring the beer
That Jenny was Shock'd and Astonish'd to hear
'I'll wager a groat to anyones shilling
I can go toe-to-toe with the landlord at Milling.
For he's naught but a fighter who's long past his prime!
And to take all your money, it won't be no Crime!'
She knew it was Him as she peek'd in the Snug
The Highwayman turn'd and she let fall the jug
With a Start, for she knew that in all of her Life
To a Prettier youth she could ne'er be a wife!
He was handsome and Dark with a scar on his cheek
At the thought of his Pistol full-cock, she went weak.
So Quick as a Flash, Jenny hatch'd out a plot
The outcome of which would be Tyein' the Knot.

'I'll wager Ten Pounds to anyone's penny
You'll not last a minute' said bold Little Jenny.
The Highwayman's face on rememb'ring the girl
Was enough to make e'en a watch-spring uncurl.
Jack knew right away he'd been 'Nabbed by the mort'
He'd be thrown in The Clink due to bragging and Port.

And yet a large part of him didn't much care
As he gazed at the maiden before him so Fair.

For the Life of a Land Pirate's merry but short
And 'tis only a matter of Time 'fore you're caught
And the last ride you take's on the Three-Leggéd Mare
Then its down from the Gallows to Lucifer's Lair.

'If I should lose the Fight, promise me this
I'll at least be rewarded by you – with a Kiss.'
Jack said with a smile, as he took off his shirt
'Now 'tis your turn to strip' said Jen, being Pert.
And so 'Up to the Scratch' went Jack Fox with a grin
And Jen's father proceeded to Bash his head in.
When he finally came-to, he'd accepted his Fate
And thus Jenny got Married and Jacky went Straight.

The moral is this: To all lusty young Cocks
If visiting Bristol, then learn how to box!

Miranda Lewis
Miranda Lewis works as a freelance editor and copywriter. She began to write fiction after attending a course at London's City Lit and since then several magazines, including *The London Magazine* and *Cadenza*, have published her short stories. She is based now in Oxford with her partner and three children.

Ground

Miranda Lewis

The boy screamed every night, often at three thirty in moments of blue silence that marked the first sign of a summer day. It was peaceful then. Nothing moved. As if by prior arrangement both sides slept. There were no gunshots, mortars, shells or hand grenades; no aircraft carved the sky. Even the rats were still. And that's when he awoke – wide-eyed, big howls, his thin fingers clutching air.

It was hot and clammy in the attic. So many bodies, so much sweat and bad-tooth breath. Most nights Dunja dragged an old coat up a ladder through the hatch and stretched out on the roof, tried to dream herself to days when she and Joze ambled the length of streets. School. Playground. Swings. Slide. Kick a ball. Across the park. Just like every other mother and child. Baker. Butcher. On for milk. Back and forth. Every day. Free, no need to scurry frantically from wall to wall, shadow to shadow, looking up, ever anxious, scanning skylines. And now, on the flat lead roof with no rail, parapet or chimney stack to hold her in, Dunja ached to linger once again with Joze by sunlit doors that smelled of orange blossom and fresh-ground almonds, of warm brown paper bags and sweet, crushed pastry crumbs.

Every morning in the seconds after she awoke, Dunja strained to stay with Joze. He'd be laughing, just about to run full-tilt at her. She'd crouch, reach out, prepare to catch him, whooping loud, and swing him high into the air, but they would never quite get to touch and she'd be back on the pock-marked roof with the stench of rotting flesh and cordite and charred buildings stitched into the air. And the kid with no name screaming under her.

He'd had no name from the day she found him. Unlike all the others, he wouldn't tell her what it was or answer any one she tried on him, so she couldn't coo a little pet name, couldn't whisper what his mama said. Instead, she'd curl him up into her lap, press one ear to her breast, cup his other ear in her hand and murmur: poems, doggerel, stories of ancient caves in the hills that cut down to the coast; she'd describe to him the sound of breeze on masts of fishing boats along the quay. She'd stroke his forehead, the smooth skin round his eyes, the bridge of his nose. And all the while she'd wonder at the mandalas of Joze's eyes. She'd stare at them, those sweet, dear, open eyes and that flap of soft hair flying from his forehead. She'd no idea if the no-name kid could guess her thoughts were not with him but she mumbled good days would come again. She had no hope herself.

Of course she'd hold him until his sobbings stopped, rub the palm of one hand round his ribs and centre on his heart. She'd carry on like this for ten minutes, fifteen minutes, sometimes more, until he flowed back from his fear. Then she'd slow the rubbing and hum low tunes, the sort he would have known from birth, so soft she knew he'd only pick them out from faint vibrations deep within her. Slow-note-note-the rhythm of his breath. By then dawn had always broken, and with it worries it was time to herd her children back down to the cellar.

When Dunja asked him once what he kept dreaming of and what it was that made him cry, he narrowed his flat, dull eyes and muttered miserably, 'A bird.'

She watched his fingers twitch. She waited.

'A bird falling. A long, long way down.'

'But that's okay though, isn't it? Birds love to swoop and soar.'

'Not this one. It can't fly.' The boy's finger seemed to pull a trigger. He spluttered, 'Bang! I don't want it to suffer when it hits the ground.'

Dunja had nearly thirty children at this point. She drew them in off the streets: small, lost, wandering bodies, often unable to tell her who they were or where they'd come from or when they had last seen their families. Anything they said that gave a clue she'd set down in Joze's book, along with details of where she found them, what they wore and items they carried. She was loathe to use the pages where he'd recorded what he'd sown or sketched a plant, roots and all, but knew the information was important. The book was the only paper left now in the building and she had to give the children histories in case one day relief arrived.

'Of course it matters where I find them,' she said aloud every time. 'Maybe some will survive.'

Although there were no street signs now and most of the neighbourhood buildings had been bombed and mortared into chequer-boards of crumbled walls and cavernous basement craters, unrecognisable to the majority of her children, Dunja knew exactly where she was. For thirteen years, in what could now have been someone else's life, she and her father had delivered post to doors with knockers, bells and letterboxes. She knew every metre of the ground, navigated as a homing pigeon from days when families lived in separate houses, side by side, and talked to each other as they went about daily chores.

Since then, thousands had fled their homes. Dunja and Joze chose to stay. Dunja felt Joze wasn't old enough to go without her, and she didn't want to leave her father, even though he said they should. And three weeks after the city was surrounded, just when the bombardment started and the exit roads were all cut off, her father got a fever. One of those that simply wouldn't break. He curled up on the cellar floor and faced the wall. There were no medicines left by then and although a doctor was rumoured to be dug in somewhere a few blocks to the east Dunja never found him. There was little she could do except fetch fresh water and try to spoon it into her father's mouth, or soak a scrap of cloth, wring it and use this to cool his head. They were in the cellar of their own house then, camped behind the rocking horse and her father's work bench. His tools had all been looted early on and the roof of Joze's wooden garage smashed. She'd sit on broken toys and piles of books, and talk of things she hoped might pull him through. Family things. Favourite things. Fresh-squeezed oranges. The beach hut by the dunes. The cool resin smell that slipped down from the forest. She'd recite poems, nursery rhymes, school tables, anything they used to say together. Dunja wasn't certain if her father heard or not, she simply hoped he did. She prayed. In those days she prayed a lot. But five days after the fever first set in her father died. He just stopped breathing and left without a sound. Dunja knew because she lay right next to him, staring at a point between his shoulder blades. Joze had no idea, not until he woke about an hour after Dunja had dragged her father by his feet into the street and up the slope behind their house to the city's makeshift cemetery. It seemed the best thing to do. She couldn't let him decompose with them. She didn't want to leave him in the street. She reckoned if she spirited him away, she'd tell Joze an angel came while they were sleeping and flew him straight to heaven. She didn't think her dad would mind – he certainly wasn't in his body any more; it had gone all waxy and yellow, and no longer looked like him. So she kissed him gently, whispered love and hauled him out up the cellar steps.

Now Dunja collected children. She'd spot them on bombardment days and swoop down to scoop them up from gullies and alleyways and sidewalks sprinkled with bodies and limbs. She'd walk straight along the centre of a street reciting names of those who had once lived on either side. There were no doors to take post to, but Dunja still paced the city; she no longer prayed; she no longer cared if she lived or died. And the less she cared, the more invulnerable she seemed to be. In the early days of the siege she had considered it her duty to stay alive. First for Joze. Then the children and the no-name boy. But all that changed when the sniper came.

They'd been in the current house for a whole lunar cycle when he appeared. One morning while they sheltered in the cellar, he took up in the room at the far end of the attic corridor. Dunja heard him long before she saw him. No more than the rustlings and clicketings of a creature in the eaves – a mouse, a sparrow – but she knew someone else was there. She tiptoed up to the top floor and peeped in through the crack between the door and its frame. The guy was squatting in one corner, gun across his knees. From his ragged clothing Dunja could not tell where he came from or which side he was fighting for. Of course she knew she should be wary: he could be one of them. But if he were a sniper, she never heard him fire a shot. Mostly he just sat and stared at the cracked plaster on the wall in front of him, sipped from an unmarked bottle. He had no possessions bar an empty sack, the rifle and a mangled wrought-iron birdcage, its wooden perch still tucked inside.

The man did get up and leave the end room regularly each evening shortly after dusk. For about an hour only. Never more. One night on his way back he opened the door of the room where they slept, glanced at the rows of children, nodded to Dunja, who was on the floor cradling a girl, dropped a heap of khaki overcoats and staggered off again. After that he looked in every night.

Sometimes he brought water. Sometimes a can of food. Or twists of sugar in old newspaper. Once a dozen cigarettes. These Dunja returned – she took one for herself to smoke up on the roof and laid the rest back on the floor outside his door; she thought he had the greater need. Then he left a bar of chocolate which had gone speckled white with age. He stayed with Dunja a while that night, brought out a razor blade to carve slithers for the children to eat when they awoke.

'Kind man,' Dunja told him. 'Thanks.'

He did not answer. She still had no idea how he spoke and knew she should make efforts to find out.

Then one night when the no-name boy was screaming the sniper man stumbled in, gathered him from Dunja's lap and took him to the room at the far end of the corridor. The crying stopped. After that, the boy went to the sniper often of his own accord. Dunja crept along every now and then to see what they were doing; it seemed that side by side, hour after hour, they simply sat and played with the empty birdcage. Not a word passed between them.

It wasn't Dunja's house she lived in now with the children. Nothing was left of that. On what had seemed a quiet day she'd been up to the cemetery to make sure there was soil still covering her father and when she came back half the street had gone, houses crumpled in upon themselves. Joze had been in the cellar, where she'd told him he had to stay. He hadn't stood a chance. She never found much of him. Just his lower left arm and learn-to-tell-the-time watch with footballs on the strap. She buried both beneath the apple tree at the back, the one her father had planted when she was born. It still stood. Her placenta was buried there. And the milk teeth Joze lost. It seemed the right place for his arm.

After several nights in the sniper's room, the no-name boy took a khaki coat and left Dunja and the children altogether. Still not a word was said. But from then on Dunja felt she could trust the man as far as her children were concerned and ceased to feel the same crush of responsibility. She began to take unnecessary risks: go for food in daylight, or water when they had enough to last till dusk. Of course, she found more children this way. The numbers swelled to fifty-eight. Joze's book was almost full. She walked streets inviting bullets, often sobbing. She did not know which tear belonged to whom, whether at any moment she was crying for Joze or her father. Or for both at once. This troubled her. She tried to give each his share. She needed to be fair. Every now and then, she'd blink and glance back at their present hideout – ravaged, gutted, but standing still – a lone tooth in a crumbled jaw. She'd see the sniper at the window, pick him out in shadow on the window frame. It was only when she saw a sudden flash – sunlight, metal, glass – that she realized he was spotting her and watching all she did.

Now Dunja began to visit the room at the far end of the attic corridor after the children were asleep and the sniper had returned there for the night. She'd sit by the birdcage, stroke the sleeping no-name boy and tell the stranger about Joze. How he liked to use his hands, growing corn, aubergines and avocados in their plot, how he wanted to study botany and work with plants when he was old enough. How she should have got him out when she was able. Should have left her father, or sent Joze with a neighbour. And how, now, she was filling the pages of the only book she had of Joze's with details of lost children. The stranger did not say a word and never moved, never blinked, just stared at the cracked plaster and sipped from his unmarked bottle.

It was Joze in the garden rather than the streets she dreamed of now up on the exposed roof. They were working side by side, slipping calendula seeds into the earth, covering each one with soil, filling watering cans, putting on sprinkle heads. But however much they filled the cans, however far she and Joze tipped them, no water came. In this dream Dunja began to cry – for Joze, and for her father. Tears dripped from her jaw, until Joze called out and ran towards her, arms waving, watch winking on his wrist.

'Mama!'

Her father was there as well. She felt his lips kiss her forehead, tried to blink, tried to speak to Joze, 'Hey, I'll swing you high until we fly,' and took a step towards him.

That was when the screaming started: 'Shoot!' Below, somewhere just along from her.

Yet running now to Joze through all the tints of dawn, the new-born mauves, the hopeful pinks, she knew they'd touch. And she did hold him. Gathered him to her chest, arms, watch, laugh, uplifted hair, mandala eyes and all, and clasped him tight around the ribs. They spun, as one, until the shot rang out, a crack that split the night. It spread in ripples and for an instant seemed to hold the world suspended.

Then came silence.

Blue silence, Dunja thought, as she floated, wrapped round Joze, her bare legs stretched as wings.

Dominica McGowan

Dominica lives in Belfast and has two sons and a daughter. She started writing seriously about a year ago. She is part of the Down Writers' Group and Queen's Writers' Group and is also an avid reader particularly enjoying Irish writers such as William Trevor and Brian Moore. Her short story 'The Mean Feast' recently won the Northern Ireland Education and Library Board's 'One Book' Competition, her first success in writing. It really spurred her on. Her greatest ambition is to have a book published.

Killing Me Quietly

Dominica McGowan

There had been a constant stream of visitors all day. First thing in the morning his mother and sisters came, they had taken over, carting in tray-loads of food. The house had been transformed. The table had been removed from the kitchen and placed against the far wall, a linen tablecloth brought for the purpose.

Around mid-day the neighbours began to arrive almost as soon as the body of the doctor had been delivered encased in satin-lined grained mahogany. It wasn't long before word had spread and people began to come from all over Castlehill and even the town beyond. Then the dignitaries came. The bishop sent his secretary, a tall angular man in clerical black suit. The local T.D., Jack Higgins, dropped in to press the flesh and the head teachers from the college and local schools came by.

His mother was now receiving the mourners, her cohorts gathered close about her. She graciously received the bishop's emissary, chivvying a daughter to fetch a glass of wine while brushing off the leather armchair. There was no part for Frances, his wife, to play.

'Help yourself to a bite,' his sister directed the mourners after they had paid their respects to the grieving mother and the dead man in his coffin. Frances hovered in the kitchen and, almost as an afterthought, they sought her out.

'Sorry for your trouble,' said Joe McCann, owner of the town's hotel, his bulbous neck and face red from the pressure of the ill-fitting collar and tie. What trouble, she thought.

'He'll be badly missed, a great man,' said Frank Rafferty, free for the day from the onerous task of educating the town's young.

'He always had time for you no matter how busy,' said Jonno Keenan, owner of the town's only garage, 'a great man, and a fine doctor.' They all concurred.

'I remember when my poor dear father was dying. God bless his soul,' said Joe, a hand moving to make the sign of the cross, 'he lingered for months, but the doctor always made time to call. He could do nothing for the poor man but he called when he was passing. He'll be sorely missed.'

'He will surely,' said Jonno. 'I remember well the time my back was bad. I was bent in two with it. I couldn't straighten for love nor money. Didn't he get me a priority appointment with the specialist above in Dublin? He was on that phone every day 'til they agreed to see me. A fine man. A fine doctor,' he emphasised the last. The group nodded as one. They encouraged each other, each story the superlative of the one before. The men pulled closer excluding Frances who, meeting their backs, walked to stand at the open back door.

'Do you remember the time the young O'Malley girl was knocked off her bicycle?' said Joe.

'I do surely. Wasn't I at the gates when it happened? Didn't I hear the squeal of brakes? I thought she was killed,' said Philip.

'Well, did you know the doctor bought her a new bicycle?' said Joe. 'That was kind of him.'

'Well I never knew that,' said Philip, shaking his head in ignorance. I never knew that either thought Frances, forgotten now.

'Odd, there were no children at them.' Jonno's voice was low and drew them closer.

'Ah no, it's a sadness I'm sure. Maybe if they'd had children it wouldn't be so hard on herself,' said Philip.

'Still, maybe for the best; children left without a father could be worse,' said Jonno to nods all round.

'Didn't his own father die young?' said Joe.

'He did,' said Philip. 'Heart attack or stroke or some such thing. It was the lad that found him. Now he was a hard man. God bless his soul.' Hands moved to self-blessings.

'Still, for all that, he grew to be a fine man,' said Philip, 'I used to pull his leg and ask him for his cast-offs.' A smile lifted his sharp cheekbones.

'He cut a figure alright. Dressed like the gentry,' said Jonno, 'Got his suits above in Dublin he told me. Harkins wasn't good enough for him.' Feet shuffled in awkwardness.

'Still, we'll not hold that against him.' A thin smile moved his lips. They recalled his youthful prowess on the field; photographs of him hurly in hand hung for posterity over in the hotel bar he rarely visited.

'Was he their star player?' said a small child standing insignificantly in their midst.

'He was indeed,' said Philip. 'He could beat any man on the field in his day.' A thought occurred to Jonno.

'Who'll take the young lads now? They were shaping up well for the cup.' A new debate took off, fresh anecdotes exchanged of how the now-dead doctor had interrupted potential lives of crime amongst the young.

'The mother must be very proud of him,' said Philip.

A huddle of women had gathered at the front door, bidding farewell to the departing priest.

'Will you not stay for a bite, Father?' said Margaret Heatley, the mother.

'I won't, thank you Mrs Heatley,' said the priest bestowing a merciful smile on the women, 'God's work calls.'

'Hold on there, Father, and I'll be with you,' said Jack Higgins, who having fulfilled his quota of handshakes, made good his escape in the priest's wake.

The women now gathered around the mother in the sitting room. The evening was growing cold and a turf fire flamed in the wide grate. Sally McGrath produced a photograph from her bag, an old tattered thing.

'This is my Sean, Lord have mercy on his soul, just before he was drowned.' The picture was passed amongst them.

'That's Thomas with him.' The dead man stood tall and confident, his arm around his friend.

'They were the best of friends from childhood. Do you remember Margaret?' The mother's head stayed still.

'They were both to be priests, they were together in Maynooth. Do you remember Margaret?'

'I do, I do, why wouldn't I,' said the mother, 'but that's history now. No point in raking over old coals.'

'It was a great disappointment when Thomas left. Why did he leave, Margaret?'

'Ah sure we're in God's hands but one thing you could always say about him, he never forgot his mother.' She spoke to the group, reclaiming the floor. 'Rain, hail or snow, he called to see me and often he would have some small thing. A loaf, some rashers, even though the house would be coming down with food.'

'You were blessed, Margaret,' said Sally stowing away the photograph.

'I was, I was,' said the mother.

'Frances will miss him,' said Bridie Fearon who had been silent up to this.

'She will,' the mother allowed, 'He looked after her well. But it's not the same for a wife as a mother. The mother is closest to her child.'

In the back room Thomas was laid out cold and stiff. His hands were clasped in front, the rosary beads intertwining his fingers. Visitors paid their respects. Most touched his hands; some more intimately kissed his forehead. All blessed themselves. Frances waited until the line had cleared. She eased the door closed behind her. She looked down at his still, set face. His hands were quiet now. She had asked that they leave the ring on him, a large gold bauble inset with onyx. His mother had argued for its removal, a memento of a loved son but Frances held out. The ring seemed larger on a lifeless hand. She stretched out one finger and touched the raised stone. He was wearing the new navy suit recently bought in Brown Thomas on one of his excursions to Dublin. She'd had to remove the tags before dispatching it to O'Kane's the undertakers. The fine cloth of it dignified him. She picked at some non-existent fluff and smoothed a lapel. A hurly stick lay at his side. Mourners had remarked on the poignancy of its inclusion. She walked to the head of the coffin and looked down into his face. She was still standing there when the door opened and his sister, Eileen, looked in.

'Frances, people are leaving and Mammy wants you to come out.' She hadn't realised the lateness of the hour and followed Eileen back into the sitting room.

'Frances,' the mother said to her when she appeared. 'Have you the album?' Frances was caught blankly for a moment.

'What album?' she asked.

'The photograph album of your wedding and honeymoon and other times. I want to show them to my friends.' Frances didn't know where it was, she said. Put away for safekeeping by Thomas. She'd have a look tomorrow.

'Can you not look now?'

The women made to move. The mother reached out two arms to them.

'Don't go yet. There's tea and food left. Plenty,' indicating the table where sandwiches curled and potato salad gelled.

'No more, thank you. It's late and you must be tired. You must be shattered.
'We'll let you get some rest,' said Sally including Frances in her look. 'The photographs will wait until there's more time at us.' They stretched their necks for cold kisses.

'Go you to bed now and get some sleep. We'll see you at the church tomorrow,' said Bridie.

'I won't sleep, I couldn't sleep. What will I do without him,' said the mother covering her mouth with one wide hand and pulling a rosary beads from her pocket with the other.

'Be sure he's in heaven, Margaret and remember you have three fine daughters and grandchildren to care for. Frances and you will be a comfort to each other,' said Sally patting the mother's stiff back. 'We'll see ourselves out, don't stir from the heat.'

They turned to go and Frances followed them to the front door, taking the opportunity to escape upstairs. After the women had left, she went quietly to her bedroom. She locked the door and taking off her clothes, stood naked before the wardrobe mirror.

What need have I for photographs to remember him, she thought. She traced the scar along her shoulder and saw the time he had pushed her through the glass door. She had forgotten his suit from the drycleaners. The yellowing bruises from his ring were still clearly visible on her breast and arms from the night she had stepped unknowingly from the shower to meet his anger. Punch by punch he had accused her of extravagance. She felt for the crease on her head, hidden amongst the hair. He'd complained about the dry dinner that time. He'd reached for the heavy ashtray and let her have it. The bone in her ankle had never set properly after the time he had hurleyed the legs from under her.

'You'll do it right the next time.' She saw again the spittle fly from him. A kaleidoscope of distorted bumps, shadows and colours gave their own testimony to the years she had spent with this fine man. A living, breathing photograph.

Charlotte Mabey

Charlotte Mabey was born in London in 1974. After completing degrees in Environmental Science and Palaeobiology, she dabbled in contemporary dance, amateur dramatics and stand-up comedy. But writing soon took over as her primary interest. After seven years with the BBC's Natural History Unit, Charlotte took the plunge to begin a more modest life permanently attached to a notebook. Shortlisted in 1997 for the Channel Four Young Persons' Sitcom Writing competition, she has also completed creative writing courses with the Open University. Her next project is a children's novel about space and time travel. Well, naturally. Charlotte lives in Bristol with her husband Tim.

Intervention

Charlotte Mabey

'I can help. I'm a First Aider.'

Shit. Is that my voice? I'm running towards the man on the ground. He's a mess. His left leg is twisted underneath him. His right hand, bent back along his arm. His head is lolling to one side, the visor on his helmet staring down at his left shoulder. Shit.

'Somebody call an ambulance.'

There is movement in the crowd.

'Sir? Sir, can you hear me?'

Shit. He is totally covered by his leathers. I'll have to take his helmet off.

'Should you be doing that?' The truck driver sits on the kerb; holding the boy with the football. The boy is crying. 'Should you be doing that? Shouldn't we wait for the ambulance?'

'He's not breathing.'

Is he breathing? I don't know. I have to get his helmet off. Shit. Where is the catch? How do these things work?

Click. It slides off. I throw it to one side.

Shit. He isn't breathing. His mouth is full of blood and broken teeth. I stick my finger into the mess and pull out the teeth. The blood is bubbling up. He must have bitten his tongue. I should turn him over. Should I turn him over? What if he's screwed up his back? Shit. I already took his helmet off. Had I moved his head? Did I move his head? Shit.

I turn him over. Move round to his side. I cradle his head and roll him towards me. His weight crushes my knees. Blood runs out of his mouth into my shirt. My new, white shirt. Red now. The blood stops coming. I roll him back.

'Should you be doing that?' The truck driver sits with the boy. 'His back looks fucked. Should you be doing that?'

'He's not breathing.'

He has no pulse either. Shit. What was it? Fifteen, no thirty now, pumps on the chest. Yes, that was right. To the tune of 'The Archers'. Only twice over, because it's thirty now, not fifteen. I hum the tune and pound his chest. One third down. Base of the ribs. One, two, three, four. I push down hard, from my shoulders. Nine, ten, eleven, twelve.

Crack.

Shit. Had I broken a rib? Shit. I'd broken a rib. Keep going. Seventeen, eighteen, nineteen, twenty. Shit. Can I do this? Can I actually do this? What had the trainer said?

'Can you make them any deader? No.'

Twenty seven, twenty eight, twenty nine, thirty.

Now breathing. Shit. Congealing blood all over his mouth. I wipe it with my sleeve. Tilt head. Shit. I moved it again. Keep going. Hold nose. Deep breath. One elephant, two elephant, three elephant. His chest is rising. That's good. Back to the pumping and to the Archers. One, two, three, four.

'Should you be doing that? Moving him around like that.' The truck driver sits in the shade of his truck. The truck sits where he slammed the brakes on a couple of minutes ago.

'He's not breathing and he has no pulse.' I'm really sure now. He has no pulse. I keep pounding his chest. The broken rib flexes beneath my hands.

Shit. Was that a breath? He breathes in, throws up and starts to choke. I grab him again, roll him onto me. He vomits down my shirt, my new white shirt. I'm a mess. Blood and vomit.

I hold his head. Shit. I moved him again. Still, he's breathing. That's good. What next? Shit, his back. Get him straight. Make him straight.

I roll him onto his back. Spine in line? Sort of. Shit, he isn't breathing. Why isn't he breathing? Pulse, yes. Mouth, shit. His tongue is in bits. I shuffle round to his head. Stick my thumbs on his cheek bones and pull his lower jaw up. A breath. Good. That's good. Breathing, yes. Pulse, yes. Spine in line, sort of.

I look down at the man on the ground. His jaw is pulled so far forward he gurns up at me with a sneer. I have to stay here now. I can't move now. I can't check anything else, do anything else. I have to stay here, holding this man's jaw so he can keep gurning up at me with his sneer.

'Is he breathing now? Is he alive? Should you have done that?' The truck driver is in shock. He is clutching the boy with the football. The boy has stopped crying. He is staring at the man on the ground, gurning up at me, his jaw covered in blood.

The ambulance arrives. Everything moves.

'What's your name, luv?' Paramedic, blonde, kind. 'Andy. Andy Hilton. I'm late for work. Should I go to work?'

I'm sitting on the kerb, next to the truck driver and the boy. We all have blankets over our shoulders. I can still smell the blood and the vomit. I look down. It's on my shirt. Blood and vomit. I'm still covered in blood and vomit.

'I wouldn't bother with work today, Andy. Just go home. This policeman will give you a lift.'

She's kind. She looks kind.

'You did a great job, a really great job. Now go home.'

Did I do a great job? What did I do? I can't remember. The policeman drops me back at home, takes my number, says he'll let me know how it turns out.

How it turns out? If he dies, you mean. If he dies. Or if his back is broken. Or I punctured a lung? You did a really great job, she'd said. What did I do? I can't remember now. I take off my new white shirt and throw it into the bin.

The phone rings.

'Hello, Andy Hilton.'

'Mr Hilton. I hope you don't mind me calling. My name is Olivia Graham. My son, Matt, was in a traffic accident last week, on his motorcycle, you were there, I think. You went to help him.'

Shit.

'I just wanted to ring, to speak with you, to let you know. You really mustn't blame yourself. Have they rung you already? Did the police call you already?'

No. Shit. No. Why hadn't they rung?

'No. Nobody's called me. Should they have called me?'

'Well, I don't know. I don't know how much they get involved. I just wanted to ring you myself, to thank you. I wanted to speak with you myself. Matt woke up on Tuesday, he's doing very well and the doctors are very hopeful.'

Hopeful? Shit.

'They've reconstructed his hand and his leg has been realigned so the breaks should heal quite normally. As for his back, well, we'll just have to wait and see.'

'Wait and see. Right. So it was...'

'Broken. Yes. His back was broken and one of the ribs was pulled away. But they have him in traction now, and they're quite hopeful.'

'Right. Hopeful.' Shit. Shit. What did I do? I can't remember.

'You're a wonderful person, Mr Hilton. My son is alive and that's all because of you. You really mustn't blame yourself.'

She'd said that twice now.

'The doctors are very hopeful. You did the most wonderful job. You saved my son's life. I just wanted to ring you, to speak with you myself. I wanted to thank you.'

'Right. That's good. That's really great. He's alive. That's good. Thank you for calling.'

I put the phone down and sink into a chair.

Shit. What did I do? I try to remember. I'd taken his helmet off. I'd rolled him over, *twice*. I tilted his head. I broke that rib. I remember the crack. But I saved his life. Yes, I did that. You can't make them any deader, right? I didn't *have* a choice, did I? Did I have a choice?

I'm walking to work, down the blood and vomit road. That's what it is called now, the blood and vomit road. I can smile when I say it.

It's a sunny day. The tops of the cars flash sunlight back at me as they pass. The traffic edges forward, past the lights, still flashing at the crossing.

Kids are walking to school with their parents. They laugh at the ants on the ground, crawling around the paving slabs. A lady in a striped dress posts a letter into the red pillar box.

It's ok. I'm ok. I no longer throw up in the mornings. And I am walking to work in the sunshine.

I roll up my shirtsleeves to feel the warmth on my arms. The cuffs are fraying. Time to buy a new shirt.

Shit. What was that?

The noise splits my ears. It pulls everyone back. Mums grab kids. Kids start crying.

A car has turned badly, hit a lamppost head on. The driver opens the door, tries to get out. She is wobbling, unstable, covered in blood.

Shit.

Sнıт.

All I can hear is my heart, beating fear into my ears.

'Wait. Please, I can help.'

That's my voice.

Ian Madden
Ian Madden's short fiction has appeared in *Carve* magazine,
the *Bridport Prize 2005* and *The Light That Remains and Other
Stories* (Leaf Books, 2007). He studied on the M.Litt Creative
Writing programme at St Andrews University. He currently
works for a company which prospects for oil in the Libyan
desert. He lives in Tripoli.

A Peddler of Sorts

Ian Madden

Those of us lucky enough to be in a classroom on the second floor could watch
its progress from afar. While reciting verb endings learned the night before we'd
steal glances into the distance as the odd cargo approached.

Even Miss McRae, a couple of crustacea per earlobe, allowed herself a
discreet peer towards the sight wending its way towards us. Emerging from
between earth and sky it came into view followed by a muddy Land Rover, Mrs
Kerracher purposeful behind the wheel.

Given the position of the island it would have made more sense for us to have
been learning Norwegian or Icelandic. But Britain had just joined the Common
Market, so *je-tu-il-elle-nous-vous-ils-elles* it was. The junior school was at the island's
southern tip. The visitor was travelling from the northernmost point. That meant
a lot of twists and turns, ups and downs; and wind – sometimes coming so
sheer and horizontal that a vehicle could be blown onto its side. In those days a
variety of merchants still drove their wares to customers in remote parts. Some
tradesmen came from neighbouring islands. Three or four even made the trip
from the mainland. 'Delivered to Your Door' was a common claim. It was written
on the sides of most vans. More often than not the drivers wore aprons. They all
had a wooden cash box in the back. My father maintained that what was on the
back of the military-looking lorry was the most important provision of all. I had
my doubts.

Every other Thursday this convoy would lumber up the slight incline and almost to our school gate. But it veered right just in time. Its destination was next door, the big school. That was just it. There was only a matter of months before I'd have to start at the senior school and submit to Mrs Kerracher and what was on the back of that sluggish lorry.

Mrs Kerracher wasn't from the Islands. She wasn't even Scottish. She had lived briefly near Snizort on Skye. From there she moved to our island, to the big house long unoccupied at the northern tip. Up there, her home would have been the first to feel the winds blowing down from the Arctic. When she moved to the island there was just her and her son, no husband. But the lack of a husband – like the story of the delft – was something no child was ever told directly. I only came to hear it as a result of lowered voices.

Adults spoke admiringly of her. They knew she'd done battle with the Education Department and won. She had shamed a resistant officialdom into providing the island with the canvas contraption, a driver and a means of transport. Many a child could convince a parent to write a note asking to be excused from ordinary physical education lessons but no parent had ever penned a similar note to Mrs Kerracher. Colds, verrucas, athlete's foot and sundry other claims were never put before her. There was a firm, frustrating and ineffable reason behind the simple insistence that we *had to*.

So, as Miss McRae had us recite, practically sing, the declensions, we chimed along with each other and looked out of the window without losing the thread of what was going on at the blackboard. Meanwhile, shuddering in its frame, heralded by our clumsy but determined anthem of irregular French verbs, there it was: the mobile swimming pool.

Coming up for air, blowing out water was part inconvenience, part pleasure. It made me smile, it made me panic. The chlorine was comfort and threat; its stink, its blue a form of punishment if you opened when you should have closed.

'I want you swimming like seals,' she'd shout. 'Seals!'

She began to sound a bit like a seal. To hear her, to make too big a splash could have been a lapse of taste or just bad manners. Dressed for hunting, she had everything except a double-barrelled shotgun. She always looked as though she had just been arguing with someone. She was feared. (Fear, a necessary progenitor of respect among children: not the terrible thing the cagey have made it out to be since.) When a backside surfaced more often than she deemed appropriate Mrs Kerracher would threaten to harpoon it. That this threat was issued in her strangulated Gaelic made it all the more terrible.

Skill in the chemical water did not come naturally. It took me ages to be able to perform the simplest of movements; not on account of the teacher's ranting or the shortfalls in my co-ordination but because, to me, the smell of chlorine was – *is!* – indistinguishable from the stink of communal wet feet. Easing off the side of the pool felt like immersing yourself in a shimmering vat of chemically-treated foot sweat.

I didn't go to her swimming classes without a fight – a fight my mother looked like losing until my grandmother gently stepped in.

Determined not to learn the breast, the back, the butterfly or any other stroke on offer, I made an appointment to see the doctor. A large man, Doctor McAuslan sat in profile at his desk, his long soft fingers interlocked above the pad bearing the imprint of the last scribbled prescription. His room had an unchanging mixture of smells: tweed, wisdom and the white material of the screen on rollers that had been in the same position in the far corner since I was born. Maybe even before that. Convinced that I could succeed where others had failed, I didn't want to reveal the extent of my acquired expertise about punctured ear-drums but I did want to nudge this man towards a diagnosis. I wasn't brazen enough to suggest what that might be but I was desperate enough to gently overdo what I said was a strange feeling in my ear.

More than anything it was his slow, ponderous lips which seemed to listen.

'Which one?'

'This one.'

He looked concerned. (The good thing about being eleven – the good thing about being five, six, seven – is that adults *will* impute innocence.) Dr McAuslan approached with his ear-torch and had a look in. At that moment his body filled the room.

Not only did he seem to be taking up the cues, the doctor went one better: he found something in my ear that needed attention. He gave me a course of ear drops and told me to come back in two weeks with my older sister. I didn't mind the ear drops but the idea of being accompanied anywhere by my sister made me await an explanation.

I got one: the procedure could affect my balance so I might need assistance getting home. Still, if it would get me out of swimming lessons…

Mounted on the back of a lorry, its inside as glittery and aqua blue as any municipal pool, its outside military green, it had the look of a partially gift-wrapped animal pen. Unlike conventional swimming pools, the travelling one did not have a shallow end or a deep end. We could watch as it approached but the mysteries of its assemblage were denied us. The lorry parked behind the cook-house, an area off-limits to pupils. How exactly the pool got indoors was a mystery. There were suggestions at the time, each one of which was tinted with sorcery. All these years later, the answer is obvious: it must have been dismantled then reassembled indoors. But how did it come to travel in one piece rather than in parts? That has escaped explanations down the years. There's still something there that a grown-up – or this grown-up, at least – can't answer.

While the chlorination arrangements were sorted out, the pool was left on the lorry parked in the open space by the science laboratories. From the top of the stairs, we'd strain for a glimpse. On windy days Mrs Kerracher's pool sounded like a line of angry flags.

Two weeks later I went back. The doctor put a towel on my shoulder and asked me to put my head on one side and hold the kidney dish in place, between shoulder and ear. Then he went over to the sink in the corner and, with his back to me, began preparations involving hot water. His stoop lost some of its kindliness. When he turned, he was holding a syringe which looked like it was for use on a farmyard animal.

He had several goes. Each required more effort than the one before.

'I've got most of it,' he said. 'But there's still a stubborn wee bit in there that won't come out.' At this point he almost stopped. 'This is the most impacted ear wax I've ever seen in a boy your age, Thomas. A lot has come out so far. We'll have another go.'

My eyes and ears felt like they were being flushed from all angles. My very eyeballs were, I was sure, being given a rinse.

'I don't want to force it. If the rest doesn't come out this time, we'll continue with the ear drops for another week. One last try. Ready?'

I steadied the kidney dish and braced myself. There was a rinsing sound, a ringing and then another noise. It was satisfaction.

'There. Look at that. You'll hear better now.'

In a shallow sauce of now-tepid water lay the contents of the kidney dish; a pellet of fuzzy grey-brown more than half the length of my little finger and darker, more troublesome pieces which looked like bits of chopped-up anchovy.

The doctor was very pleased. But there was no talk of exemptions. Which worried me. By the time the kidney dish was emptied into the sink I realised that things weren't going my way.

Because the tides and currents around the Islands are strong and unpredictable, you couldn't learn to swim in the surrounding sea. In those days the capital (in other words, the island) didn't have a municipal swimming baths. So it was this dishevelled and daunting lady or nothing.

The only English word I heard her use was 'prevailing'. She was talking about the wind. Weather conditions occupied her, obsessed her almost. She would rage at us about the current between skerries. She would warn about the *horr harr*. (She took it for granted that we knew what she was talking about. Certainly, we all looked as if we did. When I got home I asked my father what a *horr-harr* was. Even he had to ask. It was days before he was able to tell me it was a thick, devilish sea mist.) What took the edge off Mrs Kerracher's ferocious Gaelic was its reputed origin. So local legend goes, her determination to acquire the language of the islands had its roots in a misunderstanding resulting in her being presented with a large piece of delft by the island's oldest inhabitant.

'What about the other ear?' I asked, hoping that the left might save me where the right had failed.

'Clean as a whistle. That's the funny thing. The build-up was only in one ear.'

'Will this mean...?'

'This will mean you might feel a wee bit dizzy for a while. Your parents will both be at work. Is your sister here?'

I nodded.

In the waiting room – exhausted copies of *Country Life* and *The Beezer* resolutely ignored on the table in front of her – my sister sat waiting ferociously. Steeled against the possibility of having to steady me on the walk back, she walked out of the surgery door first and, seeing that I could walk unaided, continued. Steeled in my own way against the possibility of having to be held up by her, I followed. When there was no other choice but to be seen with me, my sister always walked two paces ahead. This was no different. Except that she'd look out of the corner of her eye from time to time to check that I hadn't noiselessly keeled over. To begin with there had been a swirling sensation in my ear – the sound of a sea shell pressed to it – but nothing serious enough to necessitate any kind of communication between the two of us.

On first arriving on the island with her small son Mrs Kerracher had knocked on Widow Kirsti's door and asked if there was anywhere that offered a bed for the night. Kirsti – getting on for one hundred and still puffing on her pipe – could speak some English but wasn't used to doing so on her own doorstep. She must have looked blank because the visitor rephrased her enquiry.

'Do you know where I can find accommodation?'

Kirsti, never very forthcoming even in her own tongue, must have just *looked*. The patrician visitor then partitioned the longest word into its component syllables.

'Aye,' Kirsti declared, 'I've got the very thing.'

Off she went into the dark inside of the croft. Finally she re-emerged and held out to her callers a big, patterned, none-too-clean chamber pot.

All we had to go on as children was what we saw and heard. Or worse, what we'd been told. The refined accent – even her teeth were posh, somehow; her avoidance of English; the tumultuous hair (island squalls weren't going to force this lady to wear a headscarf); the instructions in Home Counties Gaelic and the story about the po were things you knew about the swimming teacher before you actually met her. To us, she was a fearsome peddler of sorts but one whose wares were free.

The doctor never intimated that he knew what I was up to. With his considered speech and authoritative lethargy, it was impossible to tell how much he had put together or could guess. Smarting not so much at the failure of my ploy but by the suspicion that it might have been transparent I railed at my mother that I wanted a second opinion. It was supposed to be summer but there was a fire in the grate. My mother used the poker on it as she tried to calm me with facts. 'Dr McAuslan has only left the island once, and that was to get his training in Edinburgh. And that's *quite* far enough.' Muddled into feeling oblique shame at this, I was confused but not won over. Also, her bending to stoke the fire was an unspoken remonstrance: there were things other than my concerns. But I was still outraged at having been declared fit for swimming lessons. And that I'd had my ear syringed for nothing. I felt all the more pent up because these were injustices I couldn't exactly shout about.

When my mother went into the kitchen, my grandmother held out her hand and said, 'Come here, Child.'

My grandmother took my hand in her warm, papery one. She squeezed it and told me why it was better if I wasn't excused from learning to swim. In the silence which followed I could hear the flaking grey-white kindling crackle, shift and fall.

My sister lives on the island still. She sends me the local newspaper every week. It was there that I read that the champion of the island's first swimming pool had been buried not far from her house. Smiling now at the zeal with which she passed on her knowledge of how to swim and (just as important) the knowledge of where and when *not* to swim, I saw in print the fact told to me softly in front of the fire by my grandmother. This fact had – eventually – made me brave the foot-smelling water.

Mrs Kerracher hadn't been far away when it happened. On an otherwise calm day in late summer, she had been powerless to help. He had come to the island with her. He wouldn't have been all that much older than me.

And, for all the years that were to come, from her house she would have been able to see the sea which claimed him. Its heave and toss; the terrifying changes and pitiless calm. They were there should she choose to watch them. While looking out at that moody expanse, she would, I hope, have been able to take some comfort from the feeling that it was akin – almost – to being able to visit the boy's last resting place.

Ian Millsted

Ian Millsted lives in Bristol with his wife, Elizabeth. He teaches Philosophy and Ethics and has had articles published in the *T.E.S.* and the *Journal of Liberal History*. After editing an anthology of short stories by others, *Angles* (2007), he is now trying to write more of his own fiction. He is part of the Great Western Writers group based in Bristol.

Burying The Presidents

Ian Millsted

I was twelve when my father buried Jefferson. That was twenty-nine years ago and tomorrow I'll place the stone for Clinton. It's a better tombstone than either of my parents have. Smaller, yes, but somehow grander looking. The marble helps of course. My parents never concerned themselves with the comparison but, were it not for the family trade giving me a particular interest, I think I'd be uneasy seeing cats buried with more ceremony than people.

I'd had to stay off school because of chicken pox. It's a great illness to have at that age. You have to stay at home in case you infect others but after the first twenty-four hours you feel fine. An extra school holiday really except all your friends are still in school. After the first three days Mum got sick of me being around and sent me out with Dad in the van. His first stop was the petrol station where he bought a copy of the *Sun*. He bought one most days but rarely brought them into the house. I read the sports pages while he drove and read out the scores to him. When he went in to the suppliers I started reading from the front. I made sure I'd got past page three by the time he got back. Looking back I realise he gave me a knowing glance but I didn't recognise it as such back then.

Our third stop was the White House and the lady with the cats. Her name was Mrs. Lovidge but Dad usually just called her the lady with the cats when he told Mum and me about his day at dinner. She lived in a big house on the back lane between the woods and the golf course. If I tell you that she had a rugby pitch in the front garden you'll get the idea. Okay, what she really had was a rough meadow that had two sets of rugby posts at each end and was probably about half the size of a real rugby pitch but even so it was beyond anything anyone else I knew had for a garden. Her sons were away at university and the rugby posts were already starting to lean awkwardly. I once asked Dad if Mrs. Lovidge would let me play in the field and he said he thought she'd be pleased that I wanted to use it but I never got around to asking. For one thing I didn't really know how to kick a rugby ball. My school was a football school.

On that first visit Dad suggested I come in and say hello. He thought the chicken pox was past the infectious stage and Mrs. Lovidge said she'd had it years before so not to worry. We went to the back door, which was actually at the side, and were shown into a room with chairs in but which did not seem to be either a lounge or a dining room. Dad told me to sit down and talk to Mrs. Lovidge while he went and did the job. The chairs were all wicker with thin cushions and looked well used. Only one did not have a cat curled up on it. Mrs. Lovidge went off to another room and came back with a plate of biscuits. She set these in front of me and, with what seemed like one single motion, whooshed a sleeping tabby cat up into her arms, sat down on the newly vacated chair and dropped the cat gently onto her lap.

'This is Jackson,' she said. 'She's as soft as anything.'

'You have a lot of cats Mrs. Lovidge,' I said. I knew I was expected to make conversation but was unsure what wealthy middle-agd women liked to talk about. In any case, if you see five cats in a room in a domestic house it would be perverse not to notice. The tactic worked as Mrs. Lovidge was clearly happy to talk about her cats. She had nine altogether she said. She asked if I liked history and I said I didn't mind when we did about battles and castles but didn't like the bits about how bad it was to be poor in whatever period we were doing. That always seemed obvious to me. When was it ever good to be poor? Mrs. Lovidge explained that all her cats were named after American presidents. It had started as a joke when her husband had bought her a kitten as a present and because the house they lived in was called the White House. They had called the kitten Washington and it had all gone on from then. She pointed to a ginger cat stretching itself on a chair in the corner. 'That one's Fillmore, our newest along with her brother Pierce who's probably out hunting' she told me. She also told me that the stone that Dad was putting up at the moment was for Jefferson who had lived longer than any of her other cats. It was a shame that Adams had not lived to the same day. I nodded politely. Later I looked up in an encyclopaedia and found out that John Adams and Thomas Jefferson, the second and third Presidents of the United States, had indeed both died on the same day. Mrs. Lovidge made a pot of tea and asked me to tell my Dad there was tea made if he wanted a break.

I walked along a path that led from the side of the house to a wall at the end of the back garden. The back garden was probably even bigger than the front but was more cluttered. One vegetable patch looked well-kept but the rest was overgrown. Two sheds and a greenhouse looked little used except as more places for the cats to go. I found my Dad steadying the stone he had prepared as he checked that it fitted in the hole he'd obviously just made. The words on it read *Jefferson. Son of Washington. Much loved. 16 Years.* There were four other stones with the names Washington, Adams, Madison and Quincy respectively.

Back in the van I asked Dad why Mrs. Lovidge had so many cats. He said he thought she was just too soft to have the vet see to them in time and fell in love with the kittens when they arrived, so she only let them to go to close friends or family members. Her husband worked in the City in London and got paid a lot of money and she could afford to feed all the cats so why not. Dad hinted that she paid him well for the tombstones he made and engraved for the dead cats.

I was sixteen when Lincoln died. My 'O' Levels were not really enough to let me stay on at school and Dad had often said he had enough work for two of us. He trained me himself in the engraving of sports cups and shields that were the main part of his business. I picked it up quickly and within a few months no one could tell which jobs he had done and which were mine. It was the death of Lincoln, a large black and white tomcat, that marked my full entry into the family business. It was late November and already dark when Dad took an unexpected detour down the back road past the White House. He stopped the van by the front wall and jumped out for less than a minute. I heard him open the back of the van and get something out. When we were on our way again he said, 'when you work for yourself you have to make plans for a Christmas bonus sometimes.' A few days later we received the call from Mrs. Lovidge saying Lincoln had died and would we be able to do a stone for him. Of course we could. Dad shared with me the art of poisoning a cat so that it would appear to die of natural causes. I had the decency to feel some regret but I'd never been an animal lover.

How many presidents did we assassinate? Fewer than half the deaths were caused by us. Cats die anyway and we were often genuinely surprised when we got the call from Mrs. Lovidge to say that Grant or Garfield or whoever was dead.

I will confess that my first date with Kirsty was paid for by 'accelerating' the death of an old tabby called Hayes. Mrs. Lovidge even brought out lemonade to the burial in honour of 'Lemonade Lucy', the wife of the real Rutherford B. Hayes. It was always an education working for Mrs. Lovidge. I hoped it would be some consolation that the date with Kirsty went well enough that we were married a year later. The tragic death of McKinley, a smoky grey female, helped pay for the honeymoon.

I remember where I was when I heard that Kennedy died. Kirsty and I had just got back from our first parents evening for our son Peter. We heard the phone already ringing before we got in the door. Mrs. Lovidge was more upset than usual – she was often quite philosophical about the death of the cats – as Kennedy was only just over a year old. She'd tried calling Dad first but got no reply. As soon as Mrs. Lovidge got off the phone Mum called from the hospital. We paid for someone else to do the stone for Dad. I couldn't face carving the words myself.

I continued getting business from Mrs. Lovidge. Both her gardens and the cats seemed to grow more wild as the years went by. I often took time out to mow the grass round the tombstones as the numbers grew to twenty, then thirty. Mr. Lovidge died of a heart attack which was reported from a hotel room he was sharing with his secretary. Soon after, Mrs. Lovidge called in the vet to neuter all her remaining cats. From that point they would all grow old together. The last litter had been named Clinton, Houston and Davis. She'd slipped in a President of Texas and a President of the Confederacy to avoid calling a cat after Bush junior.

Last night Mrs. Lovidge called me to confirm that I would be placing the stone for Clinton the next day. I could tell that she was suffering. I told her I'd finished the engraving. *Clinton. Loyal friend. Last friend. 14 years.* She surprised me by asking for two further jobs to be done. The last would be to engrave a stone for her. The other, to be done first if I would be so kind, was to bring her some of the same 'medicine' my father and I had provided for so many of her cats.

Lee Taylor

Lee is married with two children and lives in Winkfield Row in Berkshire. He is retired, having spent most of his working life as an account planner in an advertising agency. After retirement he trained for four years as an integrative psychotherapist. He is currently taking some time out from this training to pursue other interests, including creative writing. Lee joined Slough Writers, a thriving local group, in December 2007. 'Unfinished Business' is his first short story. He submitted it for the Slough Writers' winter competition, where it was disqualified, quite rightly, for failing to comply with the entry requirements.

Unfinished Business

Lee Taylor

Jovanovic was almost ninety when I finally met him. He lived in a small apartment overflowing with books and crowded with dark, heavy furniture. His daughter brought us coffee, thick and bitter, and a bowl of almonds.

Jovanovic was nested in a large armchair, his body cocooned in a quilt. Although he was frail, his energy was unmistakable. White hair sprouted vertically from a head that bobbed about like a demonic turkey. And then there were his eyes, great brown circles of power, flashing with the desire for argument.

He fixed me with the eyes, aware of what I was thinking. 'Yes, my dear, Jovanovic is old, but not dead.' He paused. 'It is my clients who have kept me alive this long,' he insisted, laughing. Jovanovic turned to his daughter. 'Tell her, Mischa. Tell her why I am still here and not with the others in the houses of the dead. It is because I continued to work.' Jovanovic paused and looked straight at me, removing a thin hand from under his quilt. 'Do–not–give–up!' he said, each word punctuated by a thrust from his bony forefinger and a trace of spittle. The old man had that curious ability to speak with both humour and aggression, balancing the two and leaving the listener uncertain which, if either, he meant to convey. Then Jovanovic threw back his head and began a laugh that came from deep in his belly. 'But my dear,' he said at last, 'I am frightening you and we have not even been introduced.' Jovanovic thrust his hand toward me. 'Vedran Jovanovic,' he offered. 'Vedran. In my language it means happy.'

'Anna,' I replied, shaking the thin hand. 'Anna Wright. I wrote to you from London; the Institute of Psychoanalysis?'

'Of course, of course. We have the letter, don't we Mischa? You are at the Institute?'

'Yes, I lecture there.'

'A teacher then. But you do not practise?' Again the hint of fire.

'Yes, I have a private practice as well. A small one.'

'Good, good,' Jovanovic chuckled. 'Do not give up. Ever!' The old man seemed to drift off for a moment. 'So what do you want with this wreck of an analyst, Anna? Why have you come all the way to Belgrade in February?'

'I'm a great admirer of your work...' I began.

'Anna, Anna, Anna,' Jovanovic interrupted. 'You see me in this chair. I am dying Anna. I have done my work. I have my medals and titles. I have no need of admiration, even from you. What do you need from me Anna, while I am still able to give it?'

If Jovanovic had received my letter, he had not read it. I explained that I was writing a paper on the role of women in the development of psychoanalysis. I wanted to hear about the female analysts he had known. As I spoke I sensed Jovanovic first lose interest and then withdraw. 'Perhaps you could speak about the early days,' I continued, 'when you were working in Vienna and Budapest. The origin of psychoanalysis is a special interest of mine and it is so rare to get the chance to speak to someone who was actually there and part of it.'

The old man sank further into his chair. 'My dear, I am tired of talking about the old days. I have talked them to death.' He turned to his daughter. 'Some more coffee, Mischa. Please, just one more coffee.' The light had gone out of his eyes.

At this point I was sure the interview was lost. I had made the journey to Belgrade for nothing. I had been too optimistic. Jovanovic seemed to have little to give. I started to gather my things. But then something, to this day I have no idea what it was, made me stop and say one more thing. 'Vedran, perhaps there is something you haven't talked about.'

The old analyst looked at me; then over his shoulder at his daughter and then back to me. 'Perhaps there is.' His voice was very faint. 'What do you think Mischa? Is it time?' Mischa, who had said nothing since I arrived, came in from the kitchen, gave Jovanovic his coffee and placed a hand on her father's shoulder.

'It is time,' she said.

Jovanovic sat silently, looking at the backs of his hands as if trying to find something in them to distract him. Mischa passed him a thin green folder, which he opened, his bony fingers riffling awkwardly through the papers.

'I started my practice here, in Belgrade,' Jovanovic began. 'This country was part of the empire then but analysis was little known. I gave some lectures. Few attended them and even fewer stayed to the end. Eventually I began to receive some referrals from doctors. They sent me the patients that they had failed to cure or they had grown weary of, or who could not pay; sometimes all three.'

'One of these patients arrived on a hot day in late spring. He was drenched in sweat, as though he had run all the way to my rooms. I noticed the dark patches on his suit. The doctor who had referred him said he had developed a skin complaint, one that had resisted all the ointments available. The note from this doctor suggested that the patient's problem might be "psychological" and therefore more in my province than his own.'

'I was about to begin the analysis when the patient began to remove his clothing. Before 1 could stop him he threw off his shirt and turned his back to me. What I saw both appalled and fascinated me. The patient's back was marked by what appeared to be a livid burn. It was about the size of a dinner plate and looked fresh, part encrusted but still suppurating like some hideous infected tattoo. I remember the infected skin gave off a delicate smell, almost sweet, like freesias.'

'I asked the patient to dress and he did so, again without speaking. I recall wondering whether the man was mute. I gestured to the couch and he lay on his back without any apparent discomfort.'

At this point Jovanovic paused in his narrative, clearly disturbed. He let out a snort. Then he turned to me. 'My dear I should like to tell you that I explained to the patient the principles of psychoanalysis; that I discussed with him whether the lesions on his back might be caused by some somatic reaction to his mental state. Perhaps I did. If I did there is no mention of it in my notes.'

'I took my seat behind the patient and waited.

'After ten minutes the man started to speak. He was at the university studying to be an engineer. Two months previously he had joined a political debating society, one of the many springing up in Belgrade at that time. At one of the debates he had made a speech about the importance of science as a catalyst for social reform. A young lady had congratulated him on his contribution. They talked a little and went to a café. The young lady was a medical student. The two met several times after this and things seemed to be going well. The patient wrote to his mother about the girl, thinking she would be pleased. But he was disappointed, receiving a terse reply suggesting that he should not allow himself to be distracted from his studies by women and "frivolities".'

Jovanovic stopped to drink his coffee, staring past me as if lost in thought. 'The patient said nothing more about the girl, or his mother. In fact he said nothing at all until ten minutes before the end of the session. He then spoke of his ambition to be a great engineer, a man like Brunel or Eiffel who would leave his mark upon the world.

'After the session I spent several hours thinking,' continued Jovanovic. 'I confess I had not the remotest idea about his skin condition: what had caused it, or whether I could help him in any way. I reassured myself that this was only the first session of many.

'When the patient arrived for his second session he was even more agitated. He had received another letter from his mother. She had tried to reassure him about her motives. She and the rest of the family were only concerned that he succeed in his studies. After all, she had written, wasn't he the first boy from the village to attend the university? The patient wondered whether it was him or his whole family or even the entire village studying to become an engineer.'

Jovanovic looked at me again. 'I asked the patient how he felt about his mother. This disturbed him. He talked for some time about his childhood; how he had grown up feeling prized as a favourite son, yet always burdened with her expectation. I asked him whether this expectation related to his ambition to make a mark on the world. He agreed that it did. He said that once he had made his mark, discharged his responsibilities, he might feel freer to pursue his own path.

'I recall asking the patient how he would feel if he did not succeed in "discharging his responsibilities". He appeared thrown by this possibility, as if it had never occurred to him.'

Jovanovic looked at me. 'The patient agreed to come for a third session in two weeks' time. I remember as I wrote my notes I found myself drawn to the patient's use of the word "discharge". The image in my mind was of the man literally discharging unwanted desires through his skin. 1 began to feel that I might help this man, Anna.

'He never came for the third session,' said Jovanovic, closing both his eyes and the file. 'I never saw him again.'

'So there were only the two sessions in the analysis?' I asked.

'Yes, just two.' The old man paused. 'And you are no doubt thinking why has the foolish old man talked about this case? Is he senile? Has he wasted my time?'

Jovanovic let out a long sigh. 'No Anna. I have not wasted your time. This was my most important analysis.' As Jovanovic spoke his voice cracked and large tears began to fall from his eyes. The tears ran down his sagging face, dropping onto the green folder, staining it like the first rain on a dry pavement.

'The patient did not come for his third session because he had another appointment – with an Archduke, in Sarajevo.'

Alan Toyne

Alan was the joint winner of the *Guardian* and Radio 5's Young Travel Journalist of the Year award in 1997. The prize was to produce a travel article about Croatia and a short radio programme. He has travelled extensively and has written several novellas about backpacking. In 2005 he had a short story published in an anthology entitled *Bristol Tales*. He is about to complete his first novel, *Urban Ape* and lives in Bristol.

Tuesday Night

Alan Toyne

It's eleven thirty. The rain has stopped, but drops still splatter the windscreen as I drive beneath the heavy sycamore trees. The headlights pull me down the narrow lane between stone walls and clumps of bracken. The radio crackles, glows blue in the dashboard. The fuel gauge shows a third of a tank.

What if he's still alive?

The wing mirror rattles against the hedge and the passenger-side wheel churns against the bank. The lane narrows between tall hedges, a tunnel of trees closing in above me. I brake and swerve, the other wing mirror flies off and thuds come from the boot.

What the fuck am I going to do?

There is no mobile reception out here. I can't call an ambulance, or the police… The police. Fuck.

I pull into a field gateway and switch off the car. Silence. I open the door. My hand shakes.

Why me?

I'm pissed. Six pints, two vodkas. If I go to the police they'll breathalyse me. The night is full of drips from the trees. The engine ticks, warm beneath the bonnet.

I didn't hit him that hard.

I open the boot. The light comes on. I've never noticed it before, I wish it wasn't working. His head is too small. One side caved in. Crumpled like a can of lager. I can't look at it. Bone and blood. Steaming blood filling up the boot. Is his heart pumping the blood out, or is it all just draining out of him? There is a tooth hanging out of his mouth.

'You stupid fucker.' I sound like a child. 'No one walks out here at night.'

His arm flopped about as I'd rolled him into the boot, it's pointing backwards now. As if it's growing out of his back. His knuckles are puffed up and bloody. He's only got one trainer on.

Where's the other?

Back on the road. His wallet has fallen out of his pocket. I snatch it up before the black thick blood engulfs it. A set of keys jangle from it on a chain. I don't want to know who he is but I pull out his driver's licence. James Edgeson. 2B Frampton Place. When I was gulping my first pint, what was James doing? Watching telly? Ironing a shirt? Maybe he had walked the dog, left the door open and was out looking for it, worried and concerned, walking quickly up the dark lane when I tore around the corner.

'You stupid cunt.' I whisper and close the boot.

I could bury him.

That's what they'd do on telly, but some Scottish cop with a drink problem will dig him up. I can see the fucker now. Heavy fist banging on my door. Long beige coat on. Smelling of whisky.

I'm a murderer.

No I'm a man slaughterer. A slaughterer of men. What difference does it make? I killed him. I can't bury him, I don't have a spade and it would take all night to dig the hole.

Report the car stolen.

Say it has been stolen from the pub car park. No mobile reception. Pub was shut. I was going to sleep in it. Too pissed to drive and when I got there it was gone. Thought I'd forgotten where I parked it and passed out. Call it in stolen tomorrow morning.

Burn him.

Burn him and the car. Ram it into a tree. Hide the dent he made, stick him in the driver's seat and set the thing on fire. Get rid of the evidence. The forensics, shit.

What if someone sees the flames?

What if it gets put out before it's hidden all the evidence and how am I going to torch it? I'll need a length of hose pipe or tubing to siphon some fuel out. The fuel pump is fucked anyway. I'd got Derek the AA man out the other day. That might help my story, dodgy fuel pump, a crash, the engine still running. Where am I going to get a hose, I can't drive home, not if my car's been stolen? The dent will get seen. What if the Scottish cop drives past? I feel sick, get up, lean on the gate. I look for some hose on the ground. I know it's hopeless. I look at the boot. He might have something.

Frampton Place is just around the corner.

His house is dark, no lights in any windows. Two front doors, two small ones.

Bedroom flats one on top of another. I look at his licence again. He isn't smiling in the photo, not surprised; nothing to smile about is there James? There is blood smeared across the plastic, my finger prints. I've never had my finger prints taken, but the Scottish cop will do it. He's bound to. Maybe I'll get them taken twenty years down the line and they'll match them up. I'll be forty five, trembling and vulnerable in the prison showers. Why was he walking away from his house at this time of night?

What if he has a wife and kids?

I've parked with the dent facing the wall. Let's assume the arsehole has stolen my car. He comes back to his flat to get something, before he goes off and crashes into a tree. All I need is a bit of hosepipe, anything, something.

Gloves is what I need, surgical gloves.

I've got some. Of course I have. Should have been wearing them the whole time. The AA guy left me a pair if I needed to sort out the fuel pump again. I get out. Flat B. A frosted-glass door and stairs going up into the dark. The door is not double-locked. What if there is someone else inside? Headlights appear up the road.

The Scottish cop.

I step inside, close the door. The car hisses by outside. My heart pounds. I creep up the stairs, my gloved hand on the banister. My breath sounds loud, quick. Gulps of air, in and out, in and out. There is an open door at the top of the stairs, a dark silence, waiting to spring in the rooms above. I can't see a fucking thing, but I daren't turn on a light. Not yet.

A dark bedroom opposite, double bed swamped with a duvet. Orange street-lamp glow from outside juts in through a gap in the curtains. A digital alarm clock, on a chest of drawers, winks out 12.07. I hear the hum of a fridge, glance into a narrow kitchen, tip-toe down the corridor to the lounge. A couch down one wall, opposite the telly. More humming and bubbles in a fish tank. Dark bookshelves and a bean bag on the floor.

I've got to be quick.

I go back to the kitchen. The little table has shed a pile of envelopes onto the floor and one of the plastic chairs. An empty tin of spaghetti hoops is on the side board. There is a plate in the sink with a small saucepan and a couple of wine glasses on the draining board. I crouch to look in the cupboard. It's damp in there; the tap must be leaking, or the plughole. There is a pair of rubber washing-up gloves and a scourer pad in a packet, washing machine sachets and a roll of black bin liners. I go into the bedroom. The wardrobe door is open. I look down at my bloody clothes.

I'm going to have to burn them.

I open the wardrobe. A few shirts that haven't been ironed hang at one end. Not ironing then, James. What were you doing? Why were you out on the road? It was bound to happen.

Why me?

Some suit trousers have fallen off and lie tangled on the floor. I need similar stuff to what I'm wearing. I take some jeans and a tee-shirt out of a drawer. Get changed later, burn the car, burn him, burn my clothes. Then what?

Shoes. I'll need shoes, too. I look at my trainers, what if they get forensics off my clothes here in the flat? My DNA. I see black polished shoes poking out from under the bed. I pull aside the duvet and gag. A pair of girl's sandals lie next to them.

Two wine glasses.

Across the bed is another chest of drawers. I grab his clothes and go back into the kitchen, chuck them in a bag from under the sink. Take the washing-up gloves too. I still need a hose; anything will do. I leave the bag at the top of the stairs.

The shower.

The shower attachment might do it.

What if he was walking to meet his girlfriend? She could work at the hotel near the pub? Maybe she was in the pub; walking home right now.

The missing trainer.

Bending down to pick it up. Key out about to come into the flat. I run down the corridor towards the bathroom and slip, thump against the flock wall paper. A picture lies on the floor. It has fallen off the wall, hook and all. I listen. Was that movement downstairs? Is that a key in the lock? I see myself in the mirror above the sink. I've got blood on my face. James's blood and on my arm. I don't look like me, my pupils are massive, my hair damp with sweat. I look at a glass encrusted with dried toothpaste on the shelf below the mirror.

Two toothbrushes.

I see shock in my reflection and I see a naked foot. I spin round. A naked foot with blue-painted toe nails rests on the edge of the bath poking out from behind the shower curtain. I duck back out of the bathroom, snap a glance into the bath. A girl, her face broken. Blood clotting where her nose was. The shower curtain splattered with it, dried rivulets running down to the edge. She is wearing pyjamas, her hair matted and wet, blood everywhere. I can smell it. Her head twisted at an angle. All wrong. Dry black blood oozing from one of her ears, the lobe torn where an earring must have hung. 'James,' she moans.

His puffed bloody knuckles.

I look down at the picture on the floor, look at the wall, see a bloody hand print.

Not mine. His? Hers?

He's fucking beaten her half to death and was running from the scene.

What if downstairs heard?

Called the police? The Scottish cop on his way right now. Half pissed like me. He'll find me here, James dead in my boot, his girlfriend dead in the bath.

No, not dead.

Dying, gurgling. I've got to get out of here, leave her there in the bath, I've killed him and now I'm killing her too. She coughs and splutters.

I rush back into the lounge. Where the fuck is the phone? Have they got one, a mobile, what?

The phone is next to the fishtank; the two goldfish have seen everything. I dial nine nine nine and chuck the receiver down on the couch, run to the stairs, grab the bag, down the steps, out the door.

The car keys.

I rummage in my pockets, the surgical gloves bunched and sweaty. I pull the keys out and fumble in the lock. The door won't open. I've locked it, left it open all along. I climb in, turn the key. The engine chokes and stalls.

The fuel pump.

'Fuck.'

Can't call the AA out now. I scrabble for the bonnet pull beneath the steering column and hear the clunk.

I've got the gloves on so I won't get diesel on my hands.

Why now?

Why when the police are on the phone upstairs. The bonnet shrieks as I heave it open. James has buckled it. The gloves tear as I reach into the engine. I have to push the rubber cap on the fuel pump to get the diesel through, get the air out and rev the engine.

'James you fucker. You murdering fucker, get out here and help, you squashed-headed fucking arsehole.'

I smell diesel, my hands are wet.

That's what he was doing.

He jumped out in front of me. Couldn't live with what he'd done. He fucking used me to kill himself.

I slam the bonnet down. How long will it take the Scottish cop to get here? They have to trace the call. Some woman in a white shirt with a black-and-white checked tie thing will be doing it now. Head-phones on, screen winking and blinking. Getting closer and closer, pin pointing the phone call. I turn the key. The engine roars. I pump the accelerator and it cuts out again. 'Fuck.'

A light goes on downstairs.

I turn the key again. It coughs into life. The girl is lying up there drowning in her own blood. I rev the engine, rev it again. It slows, I rev and I rev and I slam it into reverse. I crash into two green wheelie bins. Glass smashes. The rear lights? A recycling crate? I swerve out onto the road.

Don't look back.

This fucker has beaten up his girlfriend. He has stolen my car. He's deranged, he's drunk, and he takes my car and crashes it. It bursts into flames. Where can I do it?

The lay-by near the railway tunnel.

Lights are coming towards me.

Drive normally.

It's a truck. The Scottish cop wouldn't be in a truck. More lights away from the road. A train streaming through the night, full of normal people, not knowing about me or James, or his girlfriend in the bath. Think, think, think.

Of course. It's obvious.

The forensics will never be able to piece it together, they'll never piece him back together. High impact, much more damage than my car. It's perfect.

It's logical.

I drive into the lay-by. Empty, thank Christ. My headlights sweep across the toilet block, cold concrete and a picnic table. Lumps of granite dot the edge of the lay-by. No chance of driving any closer.

No time to fuck about.

I chuck the torn surgical gloves into the back seat, empty the clothes out of the black bin liner. I have a roll of sticky tape in the pocket by my door, green and rubbery. I pull on the yellow washing-up gloves and get out.

Don't leave a trail of blood.

I open the boot. Hold my breath. Grab his head by the hair and pull the bin liner over the mushed mess. I have to take off the washing-up gloves, that horrible wet-soap powdery smell, to pick at the tape with my nails. I wrap it around the bin liner around his battered head.

The bushes lash my back as I drag him away from the lay-by towards the tunnel up the hill above the railway line. My feet slip in my trainers, my arm tingles from stinging nettles.

One hundred and two, one hundred and three.

I count the seconds, lose track.

Cars drift by on the road below, headlights crossing the night, can't stop now. My back aches beneath the adrenalin, my head thuds.

Seventy five, seventy six.

His legs rasp over the dry earth path, up the hill between low trees and tangled gorse bushes. His other trainer comes off. I drop him and stick it inside his jacket. People will be walking their dogs up here tomorrow; I should drag a branch behind me on the way back to rub out my tracks.

He wanted to do it. Wanted to end his life.

After what he's done I'm not surprised and he got me to fucking help him. Has the Scottish cop arrived at his flat yet, are they giving her CPR? I'm here. Above the tunnel mouth. It's got brickwork around it, ornate, like battlements. I let James roll down to the parapet and sit to catch my breath. What if the Scottish cop brings police dogs up here or his young blond sidekick with her sensible haircut?

I slide down after James.

One more push.

One more heave and it'll be over.

What if the next train through stops before it hits him?

I look over the edge. The rails gleam. He has to land right on the track. Have to get the bag off his head first though. I yank at the tape, shoving it into my jeans pocket. Bundle the binbag up and look at his ruined face.

He opens his eye.

Rebecca Watts
Rebecca Watts was born in Bristol and grew up in the Avonmouth and Shirehampton districts of the city. She attended and maintains a strong affection for Portway School and studied English at the University of the West of England. She now lives and works as a child protection social worker in Brighton. Rebecca has always scribbled stories but it was only last year that she plucked up the courage to join a creative writing class at the Connaught Community Centre in Brighton. She has never had anything published before.

Going Down Brean

Rebecca Watts

Maggie was hunched on the mud in the back garden, listlessly sifting grit through her dusty fingers.

'Beach mission tomorrow,' she commented to Kieran who was perched on his football next to her. 'You can come if you want.'

'You'd have to accept Jesus as your Lord and Saviour, wouldn't he?' Elsa called from the back step. 'Maggie has.'

'No I have not.'

'Yeah she has Kieran. She's going to get a dunk in the great big bath.'

'Shutup, Elsa. I only go because you get to go on trips,' she quietly explained.

'Do you have to sing and that?' Kieran asked.

'Yeah, Maggie knows all the songs, don't you Maggie?' Elsa interrupted. 'Come on and celebrate.'

Maggie furiously kicked out at Elsa, striking her on the shin. She suppressed the urge to kick her again as Elsa retreated back to the step, her eyes full of tears.

'Some people sing,' Maggie told him. 'But you don't have to, not if you don't want. You can just run off and play on the sand.'

'As long as you're back at the bus by four. Isn't it Maggie?' Elsa remembered.

'Yeah,' Maggie, replied, more gentle now. 'We can just play football.'

'And there's a shop to buy stuff,' Elsa approached again. 'That's where I got these jelly shoes.' She poked her foot towards Kieran.

'Yeah, alright,' Kieran agreed. 'Do I have to put my name down?'

'Ours are down already,' Elsa jumped on the spot excitedly.

'If you get there early you'll probably get on.'

'Alright,' Kieran stood and flicked the ball into his hands, 'see you in the morning.'

'Bring your ball, Kier,' Maggie shouted after him.

'Yeah,' he did not turn back as he waved.

Maggie was woken by Elsa the following morning. She blearily opened her eyes and saw her sister already dressed in a felt-tip dappled yellow tee-shirt and blue shorts, her head covered in a large, purple sun hat.

'I've got my swimming costume on already Maggie,' Elsa said and lifted up her tee-shirt to show her glossy pink swimsuit tight against her tubby belly. Maggie groaned and tunnelled under the duvet.

'Does six pounds mean three pounds each Maggie?' Elsa's muffled voice reached her.

'Yeah.'

'We've got three pounds each then. You don't have to look after mine this year. I can look after it myself.'

Maggie peeked out and saw her own red purse dangling from a thin white rope around Elsa's neck, its popper clipped shut and the name *Margaret* printed in white letters on the front.

'She left a note as well Maggie. What does it say?'

Maggie reluctantly heaved herself up to look.

'Have a great day. Love mum.' She fell back on to her pillow and looked at her watch. 'Its only 6.20 Else. The bus doesn't leave 'til ten.'

'But what time will we have to leave here?'

'About ten to ten.'

'How long's that?'

'Another three and a half hours.'

'Oh, I'll just go and wait then,' Elsa said as she backed out of the room.

They were an hour early and there were already three before them – Carly Westlake, Janine Walsh and Patrick Maxwell. Maggie knew they couldn't have their names down. They hadn't been to church since the Easter Egg service. At quarter to ten Maggie counted twenty-eight children waiting. They stood close to the kerb, desperately trying to judge which direction the Reverend and the minibus would arrive from. Elsa no longer swung her purse so brightly and her cheeks were pinched tight. Maggie wanted to reassure her but she didn't. She knew the minibus only seated fifteen, tops. Hannah, Ruth, Joshua and Joseph, whose mums all did the teas on a Sunday, didn't arrive until ten to ten and they nonchalantly sat on the wall behind the jostling throng, confidently assured of their place. There was another boy with them who hadn't been going to church long, who they called PJ. At first, Maggie had been unsure which row of the church he belonged to until she found out it stood for Peter John. Double the Christian name. He automatically joined the front pew on Sundays.

The crowd surged forward when the minibus arrived and they crammed tight against it, trying, in vain, to open the sliding door. Maggie felt anxious to join them but decided to stick close to PJ and the others who remained, unconcerned on the wall. The Reverend was trapped in the driver's seat and feebly flapped his clipboard in an attempt to bat them away. He wound down the window and was met with the full shock of their appeals.

'Sir, sir,' they cried imploringly.

'I was christened up the other church sir.'

'Carly can't come so she said I could have her place.'

'But I'm here,' Carly called from behind.

'Right. Mind out of the way, the lot of you,' a raging voice shouted from the back.

Maggie immediately recognised Rodney Chubb's mum who strode through, her flabby body stuffed tight into a polyester dress decorated with swirling, purple flowers. Her brightly-veined and knotty legs were bare and her bulky feet stomped in blue and white deck shoes. Rodney was already on the minibus.

'I'm the 'elper on this 'ere trip,' she bellowed. Her front two teeth were missing and her mouth gaped open. 'And you've all got to listen to me. Give I that.' She thrust a tattooed arm towards the Reverend and prised the clipboard from his reluctant hand. 'None of you is getting on, unless I says so. Right. You,' Mrs Chubb signalled to Joshua.

'Joshua Mundy.'

'Right, on you get,' she made space for him to squeeze through.

Hannah, Ruth, PJ and Joel were permitted to board next.

'You,' Mrs Chubb demanded as Elsa silently gulped air.

'She's Elsa,' Maggie spoke for her, 'Elsa Tanner, and I'm her sister Maggie.'

'They're both definitely down,' the Reverend explained as he smiled at them.

'This is Kieran sir,' Maggie tried. 'Our mum's looking after him today. So he has to come. Otherwise he'll have to wait on the wall until we get back.'

'That's not fair,' the others screeched.

'I really think we should make space,' the Reverend conceded. 'All the children with their names down are on.'

That was all the invitation Maggie, Elsa and Kieran needed to scramble aboard. They had to sit with their legs bent and their feet resting against the church banner and the Reverend's guitar that was lying across the floor. There were just three seats left and Carly, Janine and Patrick were approved to clamber on too.

'Right. That's it. We're full.' Mrs Chubb firmly slid the door shut. The disappointed children milled around the bus and peered through the window.

'What about that seat there?'

'That's for the sandwiches and that,' Mrs Chubb replied and dumped a box of sandwiches and two large bottles of squash on it.

'Bleedin' fuckers,' Mrs Chubb tutted to the Reverend as they struggled into the front and he pulled out the choke.

'You might have to help me with the directions Mrs Chubb,' the Reverend commented as they drove towards the motorway.

'Ain't you never been down Brean before?' she asked him disbelievingly.

'Well, no, I can't say I have.'

'Oh, it's blimmin' great down there, ain't it kids?'

'Yeah,' they all called from the back.

'We're really going Maggie. We're really going,' Elsa bounced in her seat beside her.

'M5 South, drive.'

The Reverend joined the stampede of traffic burning around them. They stayed in the slowest lane, carried along by two juggernauts belching at front and back. Their seats juddered as the minibus reached for the crest of the motorway bridge, the lorry behind threatening to flatten and outrun them.

'Lean forward you lot.' Mrs Chubb directed and thrust her body towards the dashboard.

'Mrs Chubb,' the Reverend reddened uncomfortably, 'I really don't think that...'

'What do you think I am? Soft in the 'ead? Just a bit of a laugh for them ain't it?'

Her thumb jerked to the children all bent double as they willed the minibus forward. Over the bridge Maggie could see the river, receded to a trickle on oozing mud banks and the cranes of the docks, unmanned and motionless. Maggie's eyes were scorched as she stared at the roof-tops of thousands of cars, glimmering in the sun, unloaded, parked up and unsold.

'Gordano Services, there look Rev,' Mrs Chubb pointed. 'Shouldn't really stop yet, should we?' she asked, half-hoping.

'Well, I don't think we've gone a mile yet.'

'Best get down there and make the most of the beach. Can do the services anytime.'

A right turn took them onto a single track lane that ran straight as far as Maggie could see. On one side static caravans cascaded down a steep bank and hundreds more stretched along a level plain on the other. A solitary woman washed down the windows of one. Grains of sand thinly coated the track and swirled up towards the bus.

'That's sand Maggie.' Elsa gripped the seat in front excitedly. 'Almost there.' They passed the wooden entrance to the Sunny Glades Holiday Park offering Manilow Magicke Tonite. They continued until the ranks of caravans were replaced with the concrete wall of the car park.

'In 'ere Rev.'

'Are you sure?' The Reverend frowned as he read the large sign in cautionary red and yellow. '*Dangerous sinking sand and mud at low tide.*'

'Yeah, this is it, ain't it kids.'

The Reverend inched the minibus into the car park. A small shack was huddled in the corner, inflated dolphins and rubber rings tethered to its corrugated iron flat roof. They began to click themselves free of their seatbelts but Mrs Chubb stopped them.

'None of you is getting out 'til I says so. Now. Just listen to me. Don't go too far. Got to see me and the Reverend. Ain't that right?'

'What time's the sandwiches?' Patrick shouted.

'At dinner time. We'll shout you over, won't we Rev. Then spreading the Word and the bus back after that.'

Maggie looked down at Elsa who gingerly manoeuvred her arms out of the sleeves of her tee-shirt in preparation. Mrs Chubb slid open the door and they rushed out, Elsa leading the way down the steps that led onto the beach. She tore off her tee-shirt, skipped out of her shorts and discarded them in a straggly heap while she charged, twirled and hop-scotched into the vast expanse of sand. Maggie screwed her eyes to take in the huge dank, yellow beach, broken by exposed islands of families behind billowing windbreaks. An ice-cream van was parked some way off, the man inside reading a newspaper. Beyond it, the sand darkened to a brown sludge, left-overs from the river that now lapped miles in the distance. Still further again, clouds shifted and scurried over land that Maggie knew was another country, Wales.

Kieran whacked his football to soar high over the sand. It was pummelled mid-flight and landed far beyond from where he had intended. Maggie raced after it and thrust it back to him. Elsa settled cross-legged and started to scoop out a hole with the sand.

Mrs Chubb dragged two hired deck chairs back from the shop, handed one to the Reverend and sank herself down. Carly demonstrated a run of five perfect cartwheels to PJ and Hannah. Kieran flapped his arms towards Maggie's direction and tunnelled his hands around his straining mouth, but she could not make out what he was hollering. He pointed in the direction of the car park but gave up and ran to her, dribbling the football at his feet.

'Shall we go to the shop?' he panted.

'Yeah alright. We'd better get Elsa.'

As Maggie approached she noticed that her feet were buried under two rounded mounds of sand.

'We're going to the shop, Else.'

'Oh,' Elsa looked down in the direction of her feet uncertainly, not wanting to disturb the carefully smoothed surface concealing them. 'Can you say, "Where are your feet?" Maggie?'

'What?' she replied impatiently.

'Pretend you don't know where my feet are and say, "I wonder where they could be?" and then I could surprise you,' she giggled.

'You're too old for that Else.'

'Please, just once.'

'No. If you're coming, you need to come now.' Maggie turned and headed for the car park. Elsa ruptured the sand and stamped on it before hurrying to catch them up. Maggie felt guilty when she saw Elsa regard her anxiously and she immediately regretted not doing as she had asked.

'I'll do it when we get back,' she gently offered.

'What?'

'That thing with your feet. I'll do it when we get back. You can bury them again.'

'It doesn't matter now.' Elsa shrugged and trotted ahead.

They flinched across the car park in bare, sandy feet. The contents of the shop spilled outside, spinning windmills of silvery foil stood upright in plastic ice-cream containers. There were fort-shaped buckets for sandcastles in marble blue and red and smaller, circular buckets in yellow. Next to them were two different sorts of spade. The more expensive ones had smooth wooden handles and strong metal shovels and the cheaper ones were just made of plastic. More ice-cream boxes were filled to the brim with flip-flops and jelly shoes, black pen on the side marking the size. Elsa eyed a pink rubber ring shifting on the roof.

'How much is that Maggie?'

'£1.99.'

'Can I have it?'

'What for? You won't be able to go in the water, it's filthy.'

'Just to wear.'

'Let's have a look at what else there is. You might change your mind.'

Kieran was at a dustbin filled with plastic footballs. He took out a few and expertly prodded and bounced them.

'Any good?' Maggie asked.

'Nah, not really. See what's inside first.'

It was dark inside the shop, the window was blocked by a box filled with wicker beach mats and windbreaks, and it took a few seconds for Maggie's eyes to adjust. Along one wall were sticks of chunky, hard, pink rock with names embedded through them. There were flat, red lollipops and full fried breakfasts of sugary sweets covered in cling-film on paper plates. Baskets of shells were along a second wall, rigid crusty starfish and other shells smooth and coiled. Kieran was holding a packet of Red Arrow Acrobatic Gliders.

'They do loop the loops and everything when you've put them together.'

Maggie sorted through cardboard boxes of yo-yos, hard bouncing balls and green plastic snakes that menacingly wriggled beyond her. She picked up a bottle of bubbles and tried to steer the single ball-bearing through a tiny silver maze contained in its lid. She silently dismissed the bat and balls whose rackets boomed when you hit with them and the cricket sets made from pale, sickly wood. She was tempted by the kites, neatly folded in packets, but remembered how quickly the thin cotton had tangled when she tried to launch one before.

She was staring at bags of marbles in mesh netting when she noticed something she was certain had not been there last year. The Funnyman Joke Stand. She tripped over a stray foot pump in her urgency to reach it and took in the small packets of practical jokes. Maggie supposed they were like the ones that Betty and Alicia in Malory Towers sent away to a special catalogue for. She calculated that she had enough for two and an ice cream for later. On the top rack she spotted a pot advertised as 'Invisible Ink'. Maggie thought it would be perfect for if she was ever held prisoner and her captors forced her to write a letter calling for a ransom. She would be able to write another in the invisible ink to warn people of her plight. Her mind was made up. She would buy the invisible ink and the bendy pencil. Kieran had added a bouncy ball to his aeroplane.

'Oh, wicked,' he exclaimed as he saw the 'Nail through Finger' on the joke stand and swapped it for the bouncy ball.

'Have you decided, Else?' Maggie asked.

'I could have a little think and come back later,' she suggested hopefully.

'You'd better get it now. Otherwise there won't be much time for the beach.'

'I'll get the rubber ring and a fishing net then.'

'You won't be able to use them.'

'Yes I will, I'll pretend.'

'Elsa…' Maggie warned.

'It's my money,' Elsa tried desperately. 'I'll tell mum.'

'Alright,' Maggie conceded and Elsa beamed.

The man calculated how much they owed him, writing on a paper bag with a bitten biro, his cigarette slouched in the corner of his mouth. Their coins were dropped into a metal box and with fumbling fingers he handed them their change.

'Can we have the rubber ring on the roof, please?'

He grunted and squeezed himself out from behind the counter, his pot belly poking from his vest and oily jeans falling slack around his bottom. As he shambled out he picked up a hook attached to a long pole and dragged the pink ring down from the roof. He added air from the electric pump humming by the door before handing it to Elsa, who put it over her head and hugged it to her waist.

'And a fishing net, please,' Elsa asked.

'Colour?'

'A pink one please.'

He untangled one of the whittled bamboo canes against the wall and Elsa grasped it to her and they headed back to the beach, satisfied.

'Quick Maggie,' Elsa turned to call. 'Sandwiches.' They ran to join the others who were eagerly clustered at the foot of Mrs Chubb's deck chair.

'Sit down, the lot of you,' Mrs Chubb slapped away their hunting fingers. 'There's jam or chocolate spread. Don't think you're just 'avin chocolate spread. You'll all get one of each.'

She twirled open the Sunblest bags the sandwiches had been packed in and Maggie was handed two halves, the white bread moist and stretchy and imprinted with the tips of Mrs Chubb's fingers. Maggie caught a strand of hair in her first bite and tugged it out through her mouthful. Despite meticulously brushing her hands free of sand, her teeth still crunched as she chewed. Mrs Chubb lifted the bottle of watery squash and held it between her thighs as she twisted off the lid. She swapped the bottle for a stack of white plastic cups and poured them half-full and handed one to each of them. Maggie's was gone in two gulps. There were Penguins for afters. They had begun to melt in the heat and Maggie stuffed hers into her mouth in one, the chocolate coating her teeth.

Maggie and Kieran bolted free when the Reverend started to tune up his guitar and ran in zigzags across the sand until their burst of revolt was spent. They gasped for breath together and Kieran pulled out the aeroplane from his pocket and feverishly ripped off its vacuum-packed wrapper. He hastily pulled the wings through the slit in its body and Maggie retrieved the tiny propeller that had fallen into the sand. He pulled his arm back as far as he could reach before catapulting it forward and releasing the plane to soar, spin and float through the sky. The proper Christians were standing around the Reverend's guitar singing 'Father Abraham'. Elsa settled her rubber ring on the sand and knelt outside its perimeter and started to dig a hole in the centre. As her hands dug deeper, the sand became wetter and she plucked her fishing net, scooped it down into the puddle and swung it skyward.

'A fish, a fish, a fish,' Elsa yelled.

'Is it a big one, Else?' Maggie asked.

'Shark,' she replied before plunging her net back down into the soggy ferment.

Maggie felt the remaining coins jangling in her pocket and remembered ice-cream. She called to Elsa and Kieran and pointed towards the van. The man was sitting in the driver's seat, his feet resting on the dashboard, but as they approached he rose and bent towards them through the window. As Maggie surveyed the faded, discoloured stickers stuck to the inside of the window she could hear the generator whirring. She dismissed the lollies – cola, cider, orange, lemonade, Zooms and strawberry mivvis. Cornets came in three sizes small, medium or large with flakes for ninety-nines fifteen pence extra.

'I'll have a Zoom please,' Elsa decided first. The man turned and slid open the silver lid of the flat-topped freezer and reached into a cardboard box and handed her one. There were crystals of ice frozen around the bottom and she had to use all her puff to inflate the wrapper and pull the lolly free. Kieran chose a medium cornet without a flake and Maggie did the same. They watched admiringly as the man held the two empty cones in one hand and expertly spiralled soft ice-cream into each.

'Strawberry sauce?' he asked.

'Is it extra?'

'Nah, you're alright.' They nodded as he squirted a trail of red syrup on both.

Mrs Chubb hollered them back at four. Elsa refused to put her clothes back on and Maggie gathered them in her arms. They disregarded the buckles and laces of their shoes, flattened their heels and scuffed their way back to the minibus. The seats were hot and sticky and they had to raise their legs to avoid them burning on the metal frame.

Maggie's skin felt tight and prickled with the sun and her hair briskly tangled. As the van started to shift away, the breeze from an open window budded goose bumps on her arm. At the church Kieran went one way and Maggie and Elsa the other. Elsa trooped tiredly, the rubber ring falling diagonally across her shoulder, and dragged her fishing net caked with sand. As they neared home Elsa revived and shouted through the letter box.

'Mum, it's us.'

Nan opened the door. 'Hello my lovers, I was just saying to your mother…'

Elsa burst through to mum who was ironing in the corner.

'Fishing rod, mum, look and a rubber ring.' Elsa held both up and dislodged sand onto the carpet. 'We saw the seaside and had a jam sandwich for dinner, the Reverend preached the Word and Mrs Chubb called us bleedin' fuckers.'

Tim Weaver

Tim is an entertainment and technology journalist who has written for *Sports Illustrated*, *Total Film*, *SFX* and *Edge*, and lowered the tone on The Big Breakfast and Radio Five Live. He's had a 15-minute script filmed as part of a season of shorts on Channel 4, and his first, full-length novel, *The Last Sound*, has just been taken on by The Darley Anderson Agency, who represent bestselling writers like Lee Child and John Connolly. He's obsessed with football, American TV shows, movies and travel, and his idea of heaven is sitting on a beach in South Africa with his wife and daughter.

The Close

Tim Weaver

There was a boy that used to stand next to the freeway off ramp, just down the road from the station. On my first day he was selling flowerpots, most of them white with the flag painted on the side. After a while, he graduated onto selling watermelons. After that, golf balls he had stolen from the country club down the road. Back when I first got there, he must have been about eight years old. He used to wear an old Ajax Cape Town top, too big for him, and a pair of black shorts. Some days he had shoes, some days he didn't. Some days he used to work his way down the cars, one after the other, pressing whatever he was selling to the windscreens of the cars. Some days, mostly summer days, he'd just stand under the shade of the traffic lights.

I did that same drive for nine years before he stopped coming to the off ramp. For the first few weeks after, I liked to imagine it was because he'd found something better. Something more worthwhile. Maybe whatever family he had left had persuaded him to go back to school.

Then, about two months after, I discovered the truth.

Two things will kill you here: Aids and other people. I deal with the other people. The stabbed. The shot. The raped. They're all mine. They sit on my desk – details, histories and crime scene photos, buried in identikit folders, pages spilling out where forms haven't been bound properly – and they wait for me. In the first few years after the elections, I used to assign cases to other detectives. Back then, I suppose I was in charge in something more than name.

Now things are different. Six months ago, my best detective was shot in the face after entering a township crime scene. Three weeks after that, two junior officers, fresh out of the academy, were gunned down after answering an emergency call. The truth is, some days there isn't anyone to assign cases to, because there's more people going out than there are coming in. Most of the men I spent my career with are working security jobs now – part of the armed response units that turn up at people's homes when their alarm goes off without warning. I can see the appeal of that existence: getting up every day and knowing that you're going to come home again. No machetes. No stray bullets. I've even been offered jobs like that; jobs where I could afford a house with a swimming pool and DSTV. But I've always turned them down. Not because I wouldn't want that life. I would. I'm as shallow as the next man: I want that house, that swimming pool, all the sports channels and the gated community. I know reading about the girl who's been raped and murdered in the newspapers doesn't make it right, but after all this time, it seems better than standing next to her body as blood leaks from her vagina, into the hardened cracks of the earth. The benefits of that job, of a new existence, aren't lost on me.

But I can't walk away from this.

Because, right at the bottom of the files on my desk, is the one I can't let go. Her name was Helena. She was forty-two and lived in a stunning house on stilts, overlooking the sea on the southern peninsula. When I got to the house she was lying face down in the middle of her living room. She'd been punched in the throat, and fallen through a glass coffee table. As she lay there, dazed, her attackers raped her, strangled her with a tie, and then left. On a second sweep of the house, we found that they had taken some money, and a black necklace with a crucifix attached to it. Some of the officers thought her attackers had taken it as a trophy. For me, it was more likely they were trying to seek forgiveness.

Helena destroyed my life. Eventually, she became the reason I left my home, my life in Cape Town, and moved to Johannesburg, a city I despised. I loved the Cape – the vineyards, mountains, architecture, climate, the colour of the ocean at the southern tip of Africa – but I couldn't breathe there after a while. The case became too much: I wouldn't let anyone touch it and – after a while – no one *wanted* to touch it. No one offered to help me. No one even mentioned it. It got passed over in weekly meetings, got ignored in monthly reports, and when a visiting Assistant Commissioner – remembering the initial press coverage – asked about it, he was ushered off into another part of the building to me. For me, it became a personal crusade.

There were reasons why; like the place she lived. It had 24-hour security, with two guards at the front gate and a card system at a second, and yet her killers had got beyond both – and then back out again – and I wanted to know why. The way she had died made me sick as well. She'd been invaded, beaten and forced to face down the last moments of her life in terror, while someone forced his way inside her. And I guess, one of the other reasons was that, when you're first on the scene, you feel a certain attachment to the case; as if it's yours by default.

But the main reason Helena became so important to me, why her case file never left my desk – and why I eventually left the life I knew behind – was because Helena was my wife.

I was two weeks into a new job, leading the city's homicide department. Before that, I'd worked gangs, driving daily along Baden-Powell, a beautiful, desolate coastal road that wound its way to Khayalitsha, Cape Town's biggest township. It's a vast, sprawling satellite town, except built on about a millionth of the budget of the rest of the city. Shacks mix with whitewashed one-room houses; garbage blows along the streets; there's no drainage, few street lights. People are either proud here, always looking for a way out and a way to better themselves, or they're fighting against their circumstances, trying to hit out. That's how gangs are made: anger, fear, resentment, desperation, building and bubbling away. And that's what I fed on for twelve years, and what some people believed came back to bite me.

The morning Helena was killed, I left home late, because the car wouldn't start. It was the middle of winter. Winters can be cold in Cape Town. Cold and wet. We had a double garage underneath the house, but one side of it was filled with junk – most of it left over from when our daughters were at home. After they moved to Johannesburg, one for university, one for a job, we vowed to clear it out. But we never did. So, even through Cape Town's windy, wet winter nights, I left the car out on the road. That's not the done thing in South Africa, but the car was a Jetta, not a BMW, and we both felt protected inside the vacuum of a secure complex.

Most days I wonder what would have happened if I hadn't eventually got the car started. I dream, often, about what I would do to those men if I'd been there. I imagine knuckles rubbed raw, bone pushing through the skin, bloodied. I imagine those knuckles pounding down into their faces, their chests, their throats. I imagine them lying there, dazed, and me casually walking through to the bedroom, picking up my gun, and standing there while they beg for their life. I imagine putting a bullet in their head, just as they think I'm going to spare them.

Instead, I left her, kissing her and telling her I would probably be late that night because I had a meeting about homicide stats. I can't remember whether I even looked back. Normally she stood on the veranda at the side of our house and waved me off. Normally I waved back, one hand out the window as I moved through the security gates at the front of the complex. But I don't remember doing it that day. I had a lot on my mind. Perhaps I did wave. Perhaps I didn't. I like to think I did even if, deep down, I fear that I didn't.

At the off ramp, I looked for the boy, but he wasn't there. He hadn't been there for two days. I'd been travelling that route for nine years, and he'd been there every day. Now he was gone, replaced by an even younger boy; his denims torn at the knees; his tee-shirt frayed at the sleeves. I asked him in Afrikaans where the other boy was, but he just shrugged and moved on.

And then, by the time I'd got to the station, my world had fallen apart.

I made enemies in Khayalitsha; the gangs there remembered me. The crews, the leaders, they grew to loathe me. Had this become personal? Had they found out where I lived and chosen to exact revenge on my wife? It wasn't their style, but in those first few days, I didn't particularly care. I needed to hit out at something and, in the confusion and aftermath of loss, they seemed like a good place to start. I took seven officers to the township and kicked some doors down.

It got me nowhere.

Two weeks later, I started asking some questions, but it still got me nothing. No one – not the guards at the front of the complex, not the gardening staff, not our neighbours – had seen anything. As far as the rest of the world was concerned, Helena's killer had never existed.

But then a videotape arrived.

Rumours had got out that gangs were involved in Helena's murder. Someone – probably someone on my own team – had been talking to people they shouldn't. Those people talked to other people, and other people talked to newspapers. After the gang angle started playing out, it increasingly got harder to get information out of people. They became scared into silence.

Because of that, the videotape arrived anonymously. When I slid it into the VCR and pressed Play, I could immediately see why. It was filmed by one of my neighbours from the very edge of the complex, down towards the eastern end where a small children's play area was. There were no houses down there, so it could have been anyone, and the tape had been edited down so that no one else

– no children, none of my neighbours – appeared in it at any point. We could have gone door-to-door to sweat a confession out of someone, or we could have run it for fingerprints, to see who had sent it. But, whoever had put the video in the post, had battled against their fears and still sent it. So I played the video, alone, in my office, and accepted their silence.

The video jumped a little at the start. It had been clumsily edited. Whoever had been filming had been taping their kids moments before; in the background, I could still hear them. A girl, playful screams, and a boy, trying to persuade her to climb something with him. When the footage settled, it started zooming in on my house. The door was open at the front. All I could see was the darkness inside; it was like a huge mouth, dark and ominous, and – even as I sat there, almost three weeks after I'd found her – the darkness felt like it was swallowing me up.

A breeze crackled in the microphone. More noise from the kids. A car somewhere. On the counter, two minutes passed. Then three. More wind, this time stronger, disguising the noise from the children; from the cars. Then, a silence settled across the complex. Even the kids had stopped making noise. As I watched, I could feel my hands digging into my seat; my toes curling inside my shoes; my heart pounding against my chest. I knew what was coming next.

Two men emerged from the house. One of them wiped the back of his hand on the tail of his shirt, and left a smear of blood behind. The other was still doing up his trousers, holding what must have been a stolen security card. The film zoomed in further. The guy with the shirt started to unbutton it, then threw it into a bin outside our house. He had a vest on underneath. They looked around; taking in the rest of the complex.

The cameraman ducked, and – for a moment – all I could see were the rifts and valleys of tree bark. The video jumped. It had been edited again. Now I could hear the kids, close in against the camera, whispering. Whoever had taken the footage had dragged his children into him, hiding them from sight. When the camera bobbed up again, moving away from the tree, one of the men had disappeared from view. The other followed gingerly, the black necklace coiled around his fingers.

The interview rooms in Cape Town backed onto the kitchen area. One morning, two months after she died, I looked up from the coffee machine and saw two officers bringing a boy – maybe seventeen – in for questioning. They walked either side of him, a hand on each arm.

It was the boy from the off ramp.

'Hey,' I said to him in Afrikaans. 'You remember me?'

Slowly, he looked up. He had a bloodshot eye, a cut on the left cheek and a gaunt, lifeless expression. Maybe it was drugs. Or maybe it was seventeen years living out of a shack.

'You don't remember me?' I said.

He shook his head.

The two officers glanced at me, then at him, then back to me. I could see in their faces they were wondering whether this was me going crazy. The guy who'd lost his wife. The guy who'd become obsessive; drank coffee all day; wouldn't speak to anyone about the case.

Eventually, I held up a hand to them. 'I'll take him through,' I said. 'I know him. I want to speak to him. Go and do the paperwork, and I'll take him through to the interview room.'

The two officers left.

'I passed you every day for nine years at Van Der Vaal,' I said to the boy.

His eyes narrowed.

'You don't remember?'

He shook his head for a third time. I felt disappointed. I'd always been courteous to him; always acknowledged him, even if I hadn't bought his golf balls or flower pots. Now he was staring straight through me. Just like everyone else had done since Helena had been found.

'What did you do?' I asked him.

'Stole some cars.'

'Why?'

He looked up at me again; suddenly, there were tears in his eyes.

'It's okay,' I said gently.

'I have no family now,' he replied.

'Why?'

'My mother… she died this morning.'

I paused. A tear broke free and ran down his cheek.

'Where's your father?' I asked.

'Dead.'

'Grandparents?'

He shook his head.

He wiped some of the tears away, then looked around us. A couple of the officers were staring at us. A burnt-out cop and a teenage car thief. I took his arm and walked him down to the interview room nearest to us. Inside, I flicked on the lights and pulled a chair out from the wall.

'Have a seat.'

He sat.

'Why are you stealing cars now?'

He looked at me for a moment. More tears glistened in his eyes. 'I've been trying to save some money,' he said. 'I've been stealing the cars and selling them on. The one I stole this morning... it was going to be my last. That was going to be the one that took me away from here.'

'Away?'

'The disease. It has taken my mother, my father, my grandma. Maybe, eventually, it will take me and my brother. But I'm not going to wait around to find out.'

'What about your brother?'

He looked at me.

'Can't you stay with him?'

'No.'

'Why not?'

He paused. 'He's not someone... I can believe in any more.'

'What do you mean?'

'I mean...' He glanced at me, as if unsure whether he should go wherever he was about to. Then, he reached into the pocket on his pants and took something out, turning it over in his hands. He held it up to me. It was a black necklace with a crucifix attached to it.

'I mean, he killed someone.'

I never got to find out why. Why her? Why not anybody else in the complex? Why rape her? Why take the necklace? Even as I held the brother down, squeezing his throat in the darkness of a back street, feeling his veins and his cartilage pop beneath my fingers, he never told me why. Perhaps he didn't know. Or perhaps he realised he wouldn't have been able to stop me anyway; that I was too far gone for that, even if he'd tried to tell me the truth. I suppose, in the end, a killer must recognise his reflection; the symmetry of revenge. He must have an acceptance that his sins will be revisited on him, however long it takes.

So, as long as I don't know why, I can't shut the file. It stays open, under the others on my desk, in my new office, in a city I feel nothing for. Some days I can see the necklace slipping out, between the covers of the file. And on those days I think of the brother, of leaving his body in that back street, and walking away knowing – eventually – I will be judged the same as him.

That, in my final moments, I too will look into the face of death, and know that the close will never come.

Joel Willans

Suffolk born, Joel Willans has lived in Canada, Finland and Peru. He has a degree in History and studied creative writing at The London School of Journalism. He currently works as a copywriter for a Helsinki ad agency. When not writing slogans, he writes fiction. His short stories have appeared in more than twenty publications including *Bonfire*, *Pen Pusher*, *La Fenetre*, *Southword*, *Penumbra* and *Brand* as well as several anthologies, including *The Remarkable Everyday* published by Legend Press and the *Route Compendium* by ID Publishing. In the last year, he has been successful in over a dozen competitions.

Floating On By

Joel Willans

The dawn sky was all pink and watery as I floated over the backyard, admiring the way the dew made the grass shine. It felt real nice, being so light, like I was made of feathers.

When I reached the fence I did a slow-motion forward roll and kicked off in the opposite direction. I must have got lost in the special feel of it all, because I didn't notice the light come on in Mom's window or see the curtains tugged apart.

It wasn't until I heard the window rattle open that I dropped barefooted onto the flowerbed. By the time I got back to the house, she was standing in the kitchen doorway. 'Think you're all clever sneaking up in the morning, do you? How long you been doing it?' she said.

I shrugged.

She grabbed my shoulders. 'Shrugging ain't no good. Do you hear? Shrugging don't help none. And I know that better than most. How many times have I told you? Keep your feet on the ground or your life will go to hell.'

'I'm nineteen Mom. I can make my own mind up.'

She slapped me, only once, but hard. 'Don't you dare give me any of your back talk. If I'd been stronger when I was nineteen, you might still have a pa and I might still have a man and we might not be living in this godforsaken excuse for a town.'

I bit my lip and said nothing.

She stared at me with strained hot eyes. 'I know it's difficult, Tiff, I know how fine it feels. But it will mess your head up and if you keep at it you'll never amount to nothing. Promise me you'll give it up?'

I nodded because I wanted her to shut up. She stared at me for a while longer, then stroked my cheek and asked if I wanted any coffee. Later, we ate breakfast together like nothing had happened. And all the time I was wondering if I could stop, just like that.

I'd been wondering that exact same thing since fifth grade, when one morning Mom sat me down, and told me to see if I could touch the ceiling. I'd thought she was crazy or playing some game till I started floating off her lap. She grabbed my ankles and yanked me down and started cursing. I wanted to try again, but she held me so tight I couldn't breathe. She told me I must never do it again, that it was a disease I'd caught off her. All the women in her family had it. It had ruined her life and she wouldn't let it ruin mine. But it wasn't that easy. In fact it was real difficult, especially when things weren't going too well, which was pretty much always.

She'd only caught me a few times since, but I knew how angry it got her when it happened, so for the rest of the week I kept out of her sight. Like always, I had no money, so I spent my time in the town library. In the tall, white quiet of the place I lost myself in travel books. I'd not once been over the state line and loved to read about the world beyond Dixon.

If I hadn't have been hanging out there I wouldn't have seen the advert for library clerks, and if Mom hadn't caught me floating I wouldn't have filled out an application. I didn't hold out much hope, but I had an interview and got offered the job there and then. Even when my boss, a chubby guy with eyebrows like bird's wings, let slip I was the only applicant it didn't stop me walking tall.

Mom didn't believe me at first. Then I showed her my name badge and she pulled me tight and said all I needed now was to get myself a boy and I'd be well on the way to a proper respectable life. Then she started talking about Pa and if only he'd stuck around he'd see what a fine girl I'd grown into. I let her do the talking, but I wished she didn't have to sour the day with talk of someone who'd never been anything more to me than tatty snaps and tears.

It was easy work in the library, and often when there weren't much happening, I'd stare at the painting on the ceiling and imagine how the painted angels would look close up. On my lunch hour, I'd lie on the grass outside and stare at the sky and wonder whether, if I floated real high, I'd pop like a balloon. I hoped those sort of feelings would go away, with a proper job and all, but they didn't.

I thought things would get better at home as well, but now I had myself a proper job Mom kept going on and on about how I should get myself a boyfriend. The way she talked you'd think I could just pop down to the Seven Eleven and pick one right off the shelf.

'Listen darlin', a pretty girl your age should be having themselves some fun. It ain't right you being such a loner.'

'And you'd know all about that, right?'

'It's different for me.'

She was having one of her crying days when her skin is about as thick as a bible page, so I didn't say anything more. But she must have known what I was thinking, because she shut right up and turned on the TV real loud. She gave me the silent treatment for the rest of the night.

I couldn't sleep properly that night and next morning I woke with a head buzzing with guilty thoughts. To cheer myself up, I took a different way into town and stopped off at the store for something sweet and sticky. I hadn't seen the guy behind the counter before. He had a friendly face, round and smiley and these real pretty eyes. The badge on his overalls said Jordan. 'I've seen you,' he said; 'You work at the library. You stamped my motorbike book once.'

'I don't recall,' I said, blushing. 'But there's lots of folks that come in.'

'You ever wondered how many words there are in that place? Billions, I'd reckon. Probably more words in your place than there are people in the whole damn world. You ever think about stuff like that?'

'Not really.'

'Best not to, otherwise you'll get yourself an almighty headache. Some people go crazy with thinking and dreaming too much. I think it's best to stick to what you know, what you can see with your own eyes. Like I can tell you're a pretty girl. I don't need no book to tell me that.'

I didn't know what to say, so I walked out without buying any candy after all. I ran to work, and spent the day wondering if this Jordan with the pretty eyes was teasing me. In the evening, when I got home, Mom was listening to her Elvis records and singing along so loud she didn't notice me at first.

'I could listen to his voice forever,' she said, with her eyes closed.

I nodded. I wanted to ask her advice, but I knew better than to tell that sort of stuff to her. For the next few days, I walked to work a different way, but then one morning at breakfast she started going on again about finding myself a boyfriend. Her taunting got me so het up that I took the path past the store. When Jordan saw me he hung out the window and waved at me. I ignored him, but couldn't help but smile.

I started going past the store more often. It was real nice to have someone be friendly like that. Often he'd shout out that he was coming to get his book stamped, but I'd look at the pavement and say nothing. Somehow though, he still managed to wiggle himself into my thoughts. At lunchtime when I lay on the grass, I started seeing his face in clouds.

It was a crisp, fresh spring morning, the type that makes you think that your life has started up all new, when he came striding out to the sidewalk and asked me on a date.

'Listen, I've been thinking. I see you every damn day, virtually. But I don't even know your name.'

'It's Tiffany.'

'Okay Tiffany, the reason I wanted to know is because I want to take you out. On a date. How about tonight?'

I thought of Mom's words and said 'yes'.

She gave me a big old hug when I told her and spent hours doing my nails and hair. 'You look a real beauty, a proper lady,' she said. 'Be back by ten and make sure you don't do anything silly.'

She didn't say anything else, but we both knew what she meant.

That first night Jordan took me bowling. I was so bad I almost cried, but he said there was no point getting all mad about it. Some people are good at some things and some people are good at others. I wanted to tell him there and then that I could float, but I bit my lip and nodded. I got back nearer to eleven, but Mom didn't say a thing.

They went fast, those first few months together, but it was still a mighty big shock when Jordan asked me to marry him. It felt way too quick, but I still said yes and then had to stop myself from clapping my hand over my mouth. When I told Mom she grabbed hold of me and danced me round the room and told me I was luckier than an eight-sided dice.

We found a basement apartment. It was exciting at first, getting everything perfect, decorating our little old nest in the ground, but as the weeks turned into months I started feeling heavier. And when I slept, I started to dream of floating again. It was always somewhere different, with elephants or women in funny dresses. Places far away from Dixon and from Jordan. In the morning, I'd wake up sweating and itchy with guilt.

The longer we were together, the more I found out little things about him that got me angry. He talked too much about things he knew nothing about. When I said how I'd like to go on vacation, he'd laugh and say why waste money on that when you can just turn on the Discovery Channel. And he thought because I was a woman I should do everything and he could just lie around reading motorbike magazines. Maybe it wouldn't have been so bad if I could have carried on floating, but by then all I did was hold my slowly swelling belly and wait for the small kicks that came more and more often.

After little Chloe was born, there were times when Jordan was snoring in our bed, and I was rocking the baby and watching the sun creep through the curtains, I'd go stand by the window. Opening the catch carefully so as not to wake the baby, I'd breathe the cool morning air and wonder what would happen if I just slipped out and away?

I didn't though. How could I? I had Chloe to think about and I had a proper life just like Mom wanted for me. Every time I saw her she made me make the same promise. Don't you ever do it again, she'd say. Don't throw all this away. Remember your Pa. Bolted faster than a rodeo steer when he found out. Then she'd look at Chloe and in a hushed voice say how she prayed every night the curse hadn't been passed on to the little one. I'd nod, but sometimes when I was alone, I'd take Chloe in my arms, rise up real slow from the floor and slowly swim laps of the small blue living room. And every single time, she would look at me with those big green eyes and smile.